P9-BYL-591

Remember As You Pass Me By

L. King Pérez

MILKWEED EDITIONS

The characters and events in this book are fictitious. Any similarity to real persons, living or dead, is coincidental and not intended by the author.

© 2007, Text by L. King Pérez
All rights reserved.

Except for brief quotations in critical articles or reviews, no part of this book may be reproduced in any manner without prior written permission from the publisher: Milkweed Editions, 1011 Washington Avenue South, Suite 300, Minneapolis, Minnesota 55415.
(800) 520-6455
www.milkweed.org

Published 2007 by Milkweed Editions
Printed in Canada
Cover design by Brad Norr
Cover photo: Getty Images
Author photo by Jesse A. Pérez
Interior design by Wendy Holdman
The text of this book is set in Apollo.
07 08 09 10 11 5 4 3 2 1
First Edition

Milkweed Editions, a nonprofit publisher, gratefully acknowledges sustaining support from Emilie and Henry Buchwald; the Bush Foundation; the Patrick and Aimee Butler Family Foundation; CarVal Investors; the Timothy and Tara Clark Family Charitable Fund; the Dougherty Family Foundation; the Ecolab Foundation; the General Mills Foundation; the Claire Giannini Fund; John and Joanne Gordon; William and Jeanne Grandy; the Jerome Foundation; Dorothy Kaplan Light and Ernest Light; Constance B. Kunin; Marshall BankFirst Corp.; Sanders and Tasha Marvin; the May Department Stores Company Foundation; the McKnight Foundation; a grant from the Minnesota State Arts Board, through an appropriation by the Minnesota State Legislature, a grant from the National Endowment for the Arts, and private funders; an award from the National Endowment for the Arts, which believes that a great nation deserves great art; the Navarre Corporation; Debbie Reynolds; the St. Paul Travelers Foundation; Ellen and Sheldon Sturgis; the Target Foundation; the Gertrude Sexton Thompson Charitable Trust (George R. A. Johnson, Trustee); the James R. Thorpe Foundation; the Toro Foundation; Moira and John Turner; United Parcel Service; Joanne and Phil Von Blon; Kathleen and Bill Wanner; Serene and Christopher Warren; the W. M. Foundation; and the Xcel Energy Foundation.

Excerpts from this novel were previously published in the *Dallas Morning News*.

Library of Congress
Cataloging-in-Publication Data

Pérez, L. King.
    Remember as you pass me by /
L. King Perez. — 1st ed.
        p. cm.
    Summary: In small-town Texas in the mid-1950s, twelve-year-old Silvy tries to make sense of her parent's financial problems, a Supreme Court ruling that will integrate her school, the prejudice of her family and friends, and her own behavior, which always seems to be wrong.
    ISBN 978-1-57131-677-6 (hardcover : alk. paper)
    ISBN 978-1-57131-678-3 (pbk. : alk. paper)
    [1. Family life—Texas—Fiction. 2. Race relations—Fiction. 3. School integration—Fiction. 4. Friendship—Fiction. 5. Prejudices—Fiction. 6. African Americans—History—20th century—Fiction. 7. Texas—History—1951—Fiction.] I. Title.
    PZ7.P4256Rem 2007
    [Fic]—dc22

                                2007006377

This book is printed on acid-free paper.

MINNESOTA
STATE ARTS BOARD

NATIONAL
ENDOWMENT
FOR THE ARTS

AR-4.2/5pts LJB

JAN 1 0 2008

Remember As You Pass Me By

ALSO BY L. KING PÉREZ

First Day in Grapes
Ghoststalking
Belle the Great American Lapdog

F PER
429 1762   01/09/08   LJB
erez, L. King.

member as you pass me by

h

With love for Mama, Enid Carter King,
who once upon a Texastime, knew.

⁓

And for Luke, Lexie, and Avery Pérez,
who need to know.

LeRoy Collins Leon Co.
Public Library System
200 West Park Avenue
Tallahassee, FL 32301

Remember As You Pass Me By

Remember As You Pass Me By

"Girl, You Blind?"

Just because you're a horse shouldn't mean you can't go to parties. That's why Flash isn't invited. Duane won't be coming either because he's a boy. And my oldest friend, Mabelee, well, she's a whole 'nother story. Mama says she wouldn't fit in. And Mama may be right. Me and Mabelee have a hard time being friends 'cause we're not the same color.

Still, it makes me sick. I've known her since forever. Here I am almost twelve and walking to the post office to mail invitations that ignore the friends I like best.

Mama made the guest list for my twelfth birthday party: my grandmother Bubba, three-year-old sister Sara, eight-year-old brother Larry, and the "nice" girls from Sunday school.

"Hey, Silvy!" Out of the corner of my eye, I spot Mabelee waving wildly and motioning me over to the alley behind Keasler's, the red-brick store my great-grandfather Papa started. I can't pretend I don't see her. In that orange dress, she's hard to miss.

"Girl, you blind?" She's moving closer, staying in the shade, hugging Keasler's shadow.

"Hey," I say back, waving and walking sideways,

keeping the invitations hidden. I notice she's hiding something her ownself. She's tucked a brown, paper-wrapped bundle under her arm. "Whatcha got, girlfriend?"

Mabelee giggles. "A surprise, Silvy. For your birthday, so don't you go asking me nothing more. I've been working on it ever' chance I get. You just wait."

Suddenly I feel beyond sick—Mabelee's making me a gift when she won't be getting an invitation. Does she expect one? Can't tell.

"Um, what's new, Mabelee?"

Mabelee leans closer. "You wouldn't be interested in a quick game of mumblety-peg, now would you? Alpha's sharpening the knives now, this very minute."

I canNOT believe this. For years, Mabelee's been promising that her big brother would play mumblety-peg with us—the greatest knife game around! We'd practiced tossing knives together lots, and I've been waiting for the day she'd ask.

"Great, Mabelee! We'll wipe him out."

We scoot behind Keasler's and, at the end of the alley beside the railroad tracks, I see the old jail my grandmother calls the "calaboose." That place, all dark and cobwebby, scares Mabelee so bad.

Sure enough, behind the calaboose, Alpha's drawing a target in the dirt and laying out knives while his teenager friends watch. They prance around, thinking they're so hot. But me and Mabelee can beat Alpha for sure, I bet.

When they see me, their good time stops fast.
I get a few frozen stares, someone moans, "Aw, naw,"
and then Alpha says, "Hey, Silvy," pretty cocky. He
looks at his friends and tilts his head as if something's
settled. "Pick your weapon and state your bet."

I ease the invitations into my waistband. "How
about this? Me and Mabelee against you? Bet's a quarter, Alpha, winner take all." Alpha gulps; a quarter's
a wagonload of money. Still, he struts around grinning. I choose a pearl-handled jackknife that fits my
hand like I'd been born holding it.

"Watch this." Alpha shows me how to balance
the knife, aims his, and does so-so. His knife hits the
circle all right and sticks in the dirt, but the blade
only goes in partway.

"Oh, man," says a boy I've seen sweeping up at
the City Drug, "that's plumb sad. You off or what?"

Next Mabelee practices a few times, takes a shot,
and almost misses the circle. Her knife wobbles, but
holds.

More catcalls and hoots from Alpha's friends.
"Talent like that'll keep you in the kitchen, little
mama. You ain't getting no quarter."

I whisper, "Next time," but she shakes her head.

"I'll handle this," she says, and puts her hands
on her hips. "You most better watch out." Those boys
shut up but good.

My turn. As I dry my hand on my skirt, I spot
my grandmother peering down the alley, watching
like a hawk.

"I Cannot Believe My Eyes"

"Silvan, may I have a word with you?" Bubba says. This is pitiful; you'd think I'm a child. "Now," she adds firmly.

"Hullo, Missus," Mabelee and Alpha mumble in unison at my grandmother. Alpha's fists are clenched behind his back. The other boys sit sullen, and Bubba nods stonily to everyone.

I step out onto the Main Street sidewalk with her, and she takes a healthy hold of my shoulder. "I cannot believe my eyes," she whispers, all hurt. "What would your poor mama think? Her daughter loitering where she doesn't belong. Run along on home. And knives! Mercy."

I nod at everything my grandmother says, and then my great-uncle J. D., who runs Keasler's, motions her frantically into the store. "Remember what I said," she calls, leaving. Rushing back to mumblety-peg, I see Mim-Mim, one of the more exciting girls from Sunday school, eyeballing *every*thing.

"Hey, y'all, I'm back. My turn." A few groans and a sigh come from Alpha's friends, but I take aim. And that jackknife fairly flies, landing center-circle with the blade completely buried in dirt.

Absolute silence.

Finally, Alpha says, "Whoaboy! Gentlemen, leave this lady be." They don't even look my way, but I hear a few comments while I'm getting ready to leave: "I told you we shouldn't be messing around with no knives and a white girl." "How come she caught on so quick nohow?"

Mabelee gloats, "I guess we can die now, Silvy, on this spot. We showed Alpha, huh? Your shot was a ripsnorter!"

"You can say that again," I say, but we've practiced a lot, and knives go way back around here. Our town sits along the trace where Trammel, a knife-throwing pirate, buried treasures from Galveston to the Red River.

Now getting ready for the post office, I'm even sorrier one of my invitations doesn't have Mabelee's name on it.

"You'll have to excuse me now, Silvy," she says. "I have to tee. I've been holding it, and that's why my shot was off." Mabelee slips into the tangly Johnson grass.

Bubba says in big cities signs are everywhere: "Whites Only" or "Coloreds Only." We don't have those signs, but Mabelee knows she can't go into Keasler's to tee.

"I'll be right back," I call but get no answer. "Have Alpha pay you our quarter." Crossing the road, I head up Main Street. Even though we won, this day's worse than ever. I'm in big trouble with my grandmother, Mim-Mim's off to tell my business, and Mabelee's made me a present for a party she'll never see.

Dropping the invitations in the slot, I remember how we used to go for mail when we were little. When we got to the post office, Mabelee waited outside on the sidewalk while I went inside and said, "Box 3, please."

I head back to the alley, but no one's there. Feeling empty, I know I won't see her for days. She goes to the colored school in the Bottom; I go to the white school in town. She goes colored Methodist; I go white Methodist.

Hughes Springs, Texas, does its level best to keep me and Mabelee apart.

"Behave Yourself Today, Silvy"

Goldie, Mabelee's mama, works for Bubba, and sometimes she helps us too. Today she comes out on the porch with balloons and red party napkins. Real pretty, she's tall and skinny; Bubba says she's straight up and down like six o'clock. Goldie calls me "her girl," though we both know I'm not.

Mabelee's little package is sticking out Goldie's apron pocket, and when she gives it to me, I feel wobbly inside. Unwrapped, it's a beautiful patchwork doll with a card that reads, "Your friend, Mabelee."

Tears pool in my eyes. "I wanted to invite her, Goldie, really I did."

"Hush, chile, it's okay," Goldie says. But it isn't. Trying to make me feel better, she offers, "How's about I treat you to the picture show for my present? See one of them Cochise stories you like so much?" Under her breath, she adds, "Though what you see in that savage Indian is beyond me."

Goldie loves picture shows and often invites me. I never go 'cause we can't sit together. She has to sit in the smelly balcony, the coloreds' "buzzard roost."

"Tell Mabelee I love the doll," I say. Then I look

down, arranging my blue-dotted dress, a Keasler's special. "And thank you, Goldie, for the invitation."

Bubba gives me a look. "Behave yourself today, Silvy, you hear?"

I groan. Bubba arrived early wearing her good navy blue dress, but she looks like an Indian with a bandanna tied around her forehead to keep the sweat out of her eyes. Coming early gives my grandmother a chance to give me some party instructions, since I obviously don't know how to do.

I know her rules by heart. "Never, ever, wear trousers to town." "Picture shows on Sunday are O-U-T *out*." "A young lady has to be certain her 'drawers' don't show." She might even whip out the wrinkled old Temperance Union card she signed when she was a girl, the one that says she won't ever look at liquor. If she does that, I'll pretend to faint.

Before my grandmother can rear back and let fly with more party manners, Mama comes out on the porch. She's upset with Daddy. "I don't know where that man could be," she fumes. "I told him to get himself here early. If he's in the domino hall, I'll—"

"Don't worry about it," Bubba interrupts. "Two women are better than one man any day." My grandmother doesn't think too highly of men. She gave her own husband the boot a long time ago, but she's fond of some men. She likes Jesus because he started churches and John Wesley because he started the Methodist church.

I hear a truck grinding up Kingdom Hill and hope it's Daddy. Turns out, it's Tub. He delivers groceries for Keasler's, and he pulls into the side yard, dripping sweat and smiling. Tub always goes to the back door, like Goldie and Mabelee. Once I asked why. Bubba said, "Don't cause trouble. Some things you don't question. They come in the back way and eat in the kitchen. They like it that way." It didn't make a lick of sense.

Tub tips his straw hat to Mama and Bubba. "Mornin'. Getting ready for a party? Our Silvy's turning twelve! Hey, girl, happy birthday! Got us some sody water here."

"Just put the Cokes in the kitchen, Tubrey," my grandmother says. "Tell Goldie to ice them, please. And Tub, feel free to have yourself one. It's the hottest July I can remember, not a good month to get yourself born and start partying."

"Thank you kindly," Tub says. "Don't mind if I do." He flips the bottle cap off a Coke with his thumbnail and tilts back his head, swallowing in loud gulps.

We hear cars on the road, and Bubba says, "Get ready, Silvy," adding a few more tips on true hospitality. "Cross your ankles, not your knees. And smile."

White-on-Whiters

The Sunday schoolers start settling into porch
chairs. Fanning with church fans, they look as dull
as dishwater—eight sweaty girls, mostly in white
dresses with white ruffles and bows, white socks
and shoes. White-on-white means every stitch came
from the Fashion Shoppe.

Mim-Mim arrives with a new white fan. I greet
her warmly even though I know she's busting to tell
everybody what she saw in the alley. "It's so hot a
knife'd melt butter, huh, Silvy?" she murmurs, her
eyes twinkling. I try to ignore her. "Staying somewheres in the shade?" My heart pounds like it's
having an attack.

Then we hear galloping hooves and see pink
dust coming through the pasture. Topping this dust
storm is Duane's bright red hair. No plain vanilla
there. "Whoa, hold up now," Duane hollers, and
Flash puts on the brakes before he crashes into the
porch. Bubba eyes the dust settling on her car, and
then she raises her eyebrows in Mama's direction.
Mama shakes her head; these two are *not* invited.

I try anyway. "Bubba, do you think Duane and
Flash could stay?"

"Horsefeathers," she snaps under her breath.

Mim-Mim gets real interested, real quick. "Horse-feathers," she whispers, "who'd ever put such a thought together?" Mim-Mim loves language quirks. She also contemplates the private lives of nuns, if they're bald underneath their head things, what they *really* talk about when alone.

"Hey, cowboy," I call to Duane, who seems confused. It's obvious there's a party going on, and Duane could probably use a Coke. But no one is saying, "Rein up, son, make yourself at home." Where are the good manners my grandmother's always talking about, the only things that separate us from the beasts of the fields?

When he pushes some wilting flowers my way and mumbles, "Um, happy birthday," Sally Sue says, "MOOooo, COWboy. How romantic. Giddyup!" The other girls giggle like it's funny, and Duane's face lights up as red as his hair.

"Gee, thanks, I love wildflowers," I gulp, before he spurs Flash and gallops off.

Mim-Mim winds up again, "Y'all won't be*lieve* what happened in town the other day." She shakes her glossy mane, all dramatic with enough hair for two people. "You know, Silvy?"

I suck in my breath, ready to beg for her silence. If Mabelee were here, Mim-Mim wouldn't be saying squat.

Mim-Mim leans over confidentially. "Relax, Silvy,

my lips are sealed. Pitching knives with the coloreds just puts a little excitement in this dull summer, huh?"

I nod weakly, knowing this party has ears galore.

Mim-Mim goes on, "Just awful, don't you think, moving in over that scary old funeral home?"

"My heavenly days," gasps my grandmother.

"Who? What?" I sputter.

"The new girl, I told you," Mim-Mim says with exasperation, practicing gestures she hopes will take her to Hollywood. "I hear she's a foreigner from Alabama, and she's our age. Name's Allie Rae. She's got long black hair, wears a flower in it, and, get this, a figure like a movie star."

Midstream, Mama moves us toward cake and presents. Just as I try steering the conversation back to the new girl, I hear Daddy's pickup grinding up the hill. Mama squints toward the road, probably calculating the minutes of my party he's missed, tossing away quarters at the domino hall.

Yeah, Daddy's coming, but if he brings a present from the Fashion Shoppe, I'll just cry.

"What in Sam Hill?"

Daddy pulls into the side yard waving a bandanna, a little like the one Bubba has on her head. "Happy birthday, Sis," he calls. "May you live a hundred years."

My heart nearly jumps out of my chest. Tied in the truck's bed is a goat. I can smell him from the porch.

I run down the steps and jump into Daddy's arms. "Oh thank you, Daddy. *Thank* you!"

For weeks, I've been begging for a goat 'cause I'd seen one on TV doing tricks. That glossy animal did unimaginable things for someone who's four-legged. When its trainer said, "Sit," the goat sat down; "Roll over," it rolled over. They looked into each other's eyes like best friends.

I knew if I had a goat, there'd finally be someone interesting to talk to on Kingdom Hill, not just a rock-throwing brother and a nap-taking sister. I'd be the envy of the county, able to liven up Sunday school's Noah's ark and even the manger scene.

Now here he is, aliver and grander than I ever imagined. The goat yanks and pulls, foams at the mouth, and splatters sweat from everywhere sweat can come from on a goat. Daddy struggles and ties him to the truck's bumper. Dust fills the air. This goat is plumb beautiful.

"I think I'll just scoot on down the hill home. It's been a lovely party," Sally Sue says, eyes popping. "I enjoyed every minute of it."

Noses scrunched, the white-on-whiters begin leaving as fast as their white shoes can carry them. My party is improving by the minute. I return to my beautimous present, who cries like a treed wildcat and leaps, landing on his head. "What in Sam Hill is that goat up to?" Daddy asks, sounding wiped out.

What a fabulous, fabulous name: Sam Hill from Kingdom Hill! Almost cussing, and nobody'll know.

"Trying to break its neck, looks like," says Bubba. As she gets her purse, my grandmother gives me the same look she gives Mama over playing bridge. "Don't know what you see in a goat, girl, and an odorous one at that."

"Sam Hill's perfect," is all I can say, though he's a long way from the TV star. I untie him and hold the rope tightly. As he drags me around the corner of the house, I hear Daddy ask Mama, "Don't you think it's odd Sis's never happy unless something's farting or eating hay?"

I feel kicked. I thought Daddy thought I was okay.

He continues, "You think something's wrong with our kids? Larry lurking around by himself, throwing rocks at nothing. Sis wanting to play with nigs—uh, coloreds. The baby seems all right. Maybe she'll turn out."

Something's wrong with us? And my own sweet daddy said "nigs"! On my birthday, too.

Dying Stories

This summer of '53 is so hot it's like breathing under-water. On the radio they'll tell how creeks are drying up, cows are dying ever'wheres, and dogs aren't even bothering to lift their legs anymore.

The heat brings polio. Mama says if we stay out of crowds and don't go swimming in the lake or hang out with pigeons, we won't get polio. I'd love a trip to town for a game of mumblety-peg or a chance to meet the new girl, Allie Rae, but town's where crowds and pigeons hang out.

Thankfully, I have Sam Hill for company. Teaching him tricks isn't easy though. He's not a good listener like the goat on TV, and he's a big climber, who unfortunately eats *every*thing.

Daddy drives up one afternoon carrying a stake and chain. He grumbles, pounding the stake into the ground and attaching the chain to Sam Hill. "This better do the trick, Sis, because Lord knows, our fence can't hold him. Just watch your goat, is all."

Watching Sam Hill is easy because I love every-thing about him, even his smell. Mama sighs, "Don't tell anyone else that. They'll think you're peculiar."

(I decide not to tell her I also love the smell of horse sweat.)

When polio season eases up, Bubba's the one who takes me to town to get "socialized."

That's when I see the new girl coming down Main Street. No doubt who she is. That Allie Rae looks like all the good times I've ever imagined rolled into one. She walks with a sway. Goldie says this new white girl is floozy-bound, sure as okra is slimy.

After we introduce ourselves, Allie Rae laughs and says (right there in vain on Main Street!), "God!, it's hot enough to—"

"—fry an egg on your head," I finish her sentence.

"Righto," she answers, examining me closer with her deep, black eyes. If the heat bothers Allie Rae, it doesn't show. Her clothes look freshly ironed, and her skin is clear and dry. But her eyes are the main thing. They grab you and hold on.

She tells me first thing, in one breathy sentence, her favorite things are dying stories, riding trees, and talking dirty in disguise. "How about you, what do you like?"

"The exact same," I say, though I haven't given dirty talk much serious thought. Up to now, naming my goat Sam Hill is about the dirty-talkingest thing I've ever done. But I decide there on the spot I am willing to learn.

"I've got lots of dying stories," Allie Rae says, "'cause my mama, Willie, handles insurance for the funeral home, selling and collecting both." I'd already heard about Willie.

Rumor says that Allie Rae's mother has been widowed lots of times, and Allie Rae has no father. About half the town says Willie's a sod widow; the other half says grass widow, for sure. (You can't help wondering how many husbands Willie's put under the sod, how many are still walking around on grass.)

So it slips out: "Is your mama a grass widow or a sod widow?"

"What*ever* are you talking about?" Allie Rae asks.

When I explain, she laughs. "For all I know, Willie's both. Far's I can remember, no man's ever lived with us. Just me and her following jobs and living in walk-ups mostly."

We go to Spring Park and dabble our feet in the springs. While the cicadas are going at it, Allie Rae goes at it herself. Whoaboy, the stories she can tell. She talks about dead children brought to the funeral home, about bits and pieces of people wrapped in waxed paper who make it there off the highway. "Always get heavy waxed paper," she says with authority, "cheaper kind dudn't hold."

I giggle. My family will love this stuff. It's what we talk about—car crashes, house fires, hunting accidents. "Hey, Allie Rae, I got a great idea. Why don't you come home with me? Have a Coke or something."

"Never pass up an opportunity," Allie Rae agrees, and we start climbing Kingdom Hill. Puffing, Allie Rae comments, "Looks like you live a long ways from where things happen."

"Compared to a funeral home, I guess I do."

Mama and Bubba are on the porch swing, shelling peas. I introduce Allie Rae and when I go for the Cokes, I can hear Bubba asking a bunch of nosy questions. By the time I'm back, Allie Rae's letting it drop that last night the ambulance brought in a twelve-inch baby. She heard Carlton, the mortician, tell Mr. Tom, the owner of Cedar Barton's Funeral Home, that was the saddest thing in the world. "They'd waited ten years for this baby," he said. Mama and Bubba gasp.

Allie Rae says of course she could not pass up seeing the saddest thing in the world. So after Carlton locked up and Willie fell asleep, she rolled the bed away from the partition splitting her bedroom from the world of the dead. She felt her way through the casket room and downstairs into the embalming room. She lit a match.

When she gets to this part, she whispers. "There on a white enamel table lay the body, a boy baby with a little grayish thing and a tiny, doll-like hand curved over his sparrow chest. It was sad enough to make me want to cry."

Mama looks stunned and says, "Oh, you poor thing." Bubba actually has tears running down her cheeks.

Allie Rae says, "I've gotta go now, but I can come back anytime you want."

With this new girl, I've hit the jackpot!

Riding High, Riding Low

School starts the Tuesday after Labor Day, and
within the week, its newness has tarnished. Allie
Rae groans, "I've never seen any place as dead as
here. We need something to happen."

"Wanna ride a tree?" I suggest. At Spring Park,
Allie Rae sizes up a sapling, circling her hands around
its trunk. She takes a froggish leap and climbs halfway up. When the tree begins to sway, she bellows,
"Old Faithful, we rode the winds together!"

"C'mon up," Allie Rae yells down. "This one
here's pretty broke now. Sap must of been higher
than I thought." She torpedoes a grin to the only
other people in the park—the McAdams sisters.
Today, Miss Clara and Miss Hattie have their eyeballs fixed on Allie Rae as if a spectacle's going on.

Miss Clara's head moves back and forth with the
rhythm of the sapling. Allie Rae's face glows fire-ant
red, and her hair flies around like a windmill. I've
never seen anyone ride a tree like this before.

"Mark my words, Clara," says Miss Hattie in her
loud, old-maidy voice, "that girl's wild. If she doesn't
kill herself up there in that tree, she looks like the
type who'd go in for hugdancing."

I scramble up the tree, and we dangle our legs from the branches, holding on to a bough over our heads. Allie Rae makes a sound in her throat and spits a spidery glob at the ground. "I've seen corpses more interesting," she says.

I look through the leaves and see two of Alpha's friends walking toward the park. Allie Rae notes, "Looks like the nigs are fixin' to have a big time."

At first I can't believe what she said. I must've been only three or four when Bubba told me if she ever heard that word come out of my mouth she didn't know what she'd do. She said if I needed to use it, the polite word is "nigra," or "colored."

Here I sit, high in a tree, with the most exciting person I've ever met, hearing her talk ugly. I know I should say something loyal to Mabelee. But I don't. And I'm ashamed.

"The Pot Calling the Kettle Black"

Goldie and Mabelee huff up Kingdom Hill, fretting
with each step. They're coming to help with Mama's
Win-One Sunday school class tea. Doesn't it just
figure, Mabelee can come to Mama's party but not
mine?

Mabelee's a sight for sore eyes! She's wearing a
bright yellow dress with red sandals, and her hair
is tied up in pink ribbons going ever' which way.
I haven't seen her since my birthday party, and the
thank-you note I sent was not acknowledged.

"Listen up, you sassing girl," Goldie instructs
Mabelee as they arrive, "keep out of harm's way
where you belong, and come when I call you. And
you," she says to me, "don't let me catch you moon-
ing around with no book. You know them church
ladies will be here soon."

"Hey, Mabelee." I poke her in the side, and she
grins the same as ever. "Let's get outta here."

We sneak out back and sit next to Sam Hill, who's
chained. "Not too clean, huh?" Mabelee snorts. I
ignore her rude comment.

Goldie returns to boss us around some more.
"You two listen out for Sara. It's her naptime." Then

she lists on her fingers: "First off, behave, though Lord knows, you can't make no pound cake outta fertilizer. Pretty is as pretty does." She catches her breath and slams inside. "Be sweet."

Mabelee lets out a "Whew."

"C'mon," I say. "I know a good place to hide and hear it all." Mabelee and I are drawn to eavesdropping like cats to a flower bed. We crouch in the nandina bushes beneath the front-room window and wait. I want to thank her proper for my great birthday gift, but I'm still embarrassed that she wasn't invited to my party.

I mumble, "You know, Mabelee, that doll," when the Win-Oners drown me out welcoming each other. Miz Howell announces the afternoon's topic, the preaching of Jeremiah. The leaves on the magnolia tree are still, but electric fans try to stir up a breeze.

"Oh, me," Mabelee grumbles, not hearing me mention the doll, "Jeremiah's bad news with all that dying and exile stuff. He has hisself more troubles than us coloreds. Brother Posey says we need to watch how Bible folks handle hard times and do the same."

"'Most everybody likes Brother Posey, Mabelee. I bet if he was white, he'd be mayor."

Mabelee snickers. "A white Brother Posey! Did you know he's looking to get us a youth adviser?"

"You mean for church or school, or what?"

"Most likely both," Mabelee says. "To help with what needs helping." She sighs and settles into a nandina bush.

A youth adviser? We don't have one of those.

Inside, the scriptures fairly roll off Miz Howell's tongue. From the kitchen, Goldie calls out "Yes, Lord" in a ghostly voice every time she hears something particularly gloomy about Jeremiah.

I can't quit thinking about a colored youth adviser. "Mabelee, if Brother Posey found someone to help out at your school, you might get to have cheerleaders. Wouldn't that be something?"

"Huh?" Mabelee says. "Us cheering. For what, Silvy?"

"If you had cheerleaders, you could have sports."

"That'd surely be something." She's awful quiet then, probably seeing herself cheering in a short satin skirt at Friday-night games. Colored football games. Finally, she complains, "How long's this going on? Sitting in scratchy bushes, dirtying up my dress. Tea's longer than church."

"You want to take Sam Hill for a walk?" I suggest.

"Ex-*cuse* me? You dumb as a door? Somebody I know might see us," Mabelee says. "Onliest trash lives with goats, and Brother Posey says we are good as anybody. No trash here. Nuh-*uh*."

"The pot calling the kettle black," I say, elbowing her.

At first, her lips jut into a pout till I remind her

that *she* called *me* trash. She concedes, "At least your brother's dog is named Inky, not Nig." We go into pretty loud hoots over that one.

"The pot, the kettle, and Inky," Mabelee whoops. She puts her hands over her mouth. Too late.

Goldie's face rustles into the bushes. "They can hear you two in kingdom come," she hisses. "Miss Minnie she's crying her eyes out, just winding herself up to do a number on the piano, when you started in."

Mabelee crouches into my shoulder, but we're out of Goldie's reach. "I take care of you directly Mabelee, when I get you home, but you, you girl, is Miss Maggie-bound if I have any say."

Miss Maggie runs the School of Manners that meets in the firehouse on Wednesdays after school. She teaches you how to balance a teacup on your knees and lift your pinky while sipping. You walk around with books on your head for good posture and say good-bye with curtsies. It's enough to make you puke.

Goldie stomps back inside saying, "Miss Maggie, look out!"

Screams coming from the front room sound worse than Jeremiah. Then furniture crashes and glass tinkles.

Running inside the back door, I see a big hole in the screen. An exodus of women rushes out the front, like missionaries to spread the word.

My stomach hits the floor. In the middle of the front room Sam Hill stands, chain dangling, his hooves planted on the newly cleaned rug. Miss Minnie's trapped behind the piano bench. "Excuse me, please," she says, nodding to Sam Hill and rushing past us.

I drag my friend outside by the collar. He gives a bleat, sending goat spit flying. I never noticed how loud he was before, maybe even rude. With Sam Hill safely tied, I rush to the side yard to watch the happenings.

Mama and Bubba are by the door. Ramrod-straight posture, clear blue eyes, and light brown hair usually make them look alike. Not now. Today, Bubba towers over Mama, whose shoulders slump and eyes look empty as she calls after everybody, "Careful now. Watch those steps." While Mama watches her guests skedaddle with hardly a good-bye, Bubba pats her shoulder. "It'll be all right. In a hundred years, what difference will it make?"

It'll take a *hundred* years?

Mama starts to cry so loud she wakes up Sara. Like magic, Larry and Inky appear. When Larry sees the mess, he chuckles, "You're gonna catch it now, Silvy."

Goldie puts her cream-and-brown hands on her hips, framing her body with triangles. "Sweet Jesus," she says, stifling a giggle, "excusing herself to a goat. C'mon, Mabelee, we're leaving directly. It was a mistake bringing you here. First thing we know, you and Silvy'll both be locked in the calaboose."

Mabelee shudders. "Not that, Mama. I'll be good, I promise."

Goldie pats Mabelee's shoulder. "You know I was only kidding, chile." They leave fast enough to make dust. I hear Mabelee say, "Onliest trash kids lives with goats, huh Mama? I told Silvy, but she never listens to me," and Goldie's laugh follows them down Kingdom Hill. I sit on the bottom porch step and watch them go, Mabelee walking loose as a goose.

"I'll Take Care of Sis"

Mama and Bubba stand on the porch till Mama settles
down. Bubba tries a joke: "Looks like the Win-One
won't be winning one today."

Mama goes berserk, crying gullywashers. Then,
from scraps I hear, I know they're talking about me.
"Out of control," something, something, something,
"What . . . people think?" mumble, sob, sob, "He
should do something . . . , something, something,
something . . . , Can't go on . . . nerves are torn up."
And finally the corker, from Bubba: "Poor Maggie,
she doesn't know what she's in for."

Poor Maggie?!

When Bubba drives off, I join Mama on the porch,
intending to tell her how sorry I am. And I am. Before
I can open my mouth, Mama says in a funnel-cloud
voice, "Go get your switch, a big one."

I hate having to get my own switch.

"On second thought," Mama adds, "I think we'll
let your father handle this. You go to your room and
stay there." Her eyes match her voice, swirling and
wild.

In my room, holding a glass to the wall, I can
hear Mama on the phone. "Come home NOW," she

shouts, and then she bangs the receiver. Her sobbing starts over.

I wait, knowing Daddy will get a full report.

Daddy doesn't come.

And he doesn't come.

And doesn't come.

I hear Mama on the phone again. "Are you sure? What time? I need him home. Tell him if—" Once more she crashes the receiver.

The window goes from late afternoon to evening to nearly dark before I hear Daddy's pickup.

Mama starts in right away. She yells and cries and yells some more. She tells Daddy she never treated *her* mother this way, says daughters should be a comfort.

For the first time, Daddy yells back. His voice thunders through the house. "I *told* you we had no business getting Sam Hill. What can you expect living with a goat, hanging out with coloreds?" he shouts.

Mama's conniption begins sounding like a whimper. "You shouldn't talk like that," she says, settling down. "They'll all hear you."

"Don't care if they do. It's the truth. Our kids are running wild. Especially Sis."

"So you've gotten yourself out of the domino hall and noticed?"

"Don't change the subject," Daddy fairly roars. "No matter what, I can't please you. Ever. Or your mother. You know, you seemed happier when you played bridge."

"Bridge is over, okay. That revival preacher made me see what Mother always said. Cards take too much time away from my family."

Daddy says, "As far as that's concerned, he was just some two-bit evangelist peddling guilt." Then in his sweetest voice, "You should ease up on yourself." I picture Daddy patting Mama's hand. "You're a good woman, and you don't need some fire-breathing preacher telling you otherwise."

For all she says, Mama could be a dust mop.

"You lie down. I'll take care of Sis," Daddy says.

I can see Mama lying with a rag on her head. All because of me, the daughter who is no comfort.

Daddy bangs open my door and begins taking off his belt. "You're in big trouble, Sis, embarrassing your poor mama like that. I'm gonna jerk a knot upside your head."

He slams the door and starts toward me. Daddy raises his belt, and his eyes glare. The veins on his neck stand out. Then he wipes his sweaty forehead. "Jump around and yell," he whispers, "like you mean it."

"What?"

"Oh for pity sakes! For once, do as I tell you," he says, "no lip." Daddy begins thrashing my bed with his belt.

The belt rises and falls, and I yell like a stuck pig.

"Ow, stop it, that *hurts*," I cry. "Stop. Please, Daddy, I'll be good. Forever. It won't happen again."

"That's for damn sure," Daddy pants. "It better not." He whispers, "Pinch your legs. Hard."

I begin pinching for all I am worth, even slap myself a few times.

"Don't overdo it, no need to get pitiful." After a few more bed whacks, my whipping is over. I spit on my fingers and rub my eyes wet.

When Daddy and I leave my room, we bump into Sara and Larry. Larry's eyes zero in on my red legs. "See?" he says, "I told you you'd catch it," but he doesn't look too happy. Sara is crying with her fists balled on her eyes.

But I am still Daddy's princess.

"Ever Sleep in a Casket?"

On Friday, the harvest moon rises, and Mama's temper with me begins to wane. Allie Rae calls with an invitation. "How'd you like to spend the night?"

"Um, where?"

"Well, down here. Where else'd you think? Willie's going to an insurance convention so we'll have the place to ourselves. Providing no body comes in."

I let that idea shudder home.

Mama'll never let me spend the night with someone whose mother isn't home. Certainly not alone at night in a funeral home. "I'm not sure I can."

"Hey, you're not too scared to sleep here, are you? Our neighbors never bother anyone." Allie Rae snorts over that one; she loves her own jokes. "Besides which, Willie left me money for baloney-burgers, and the Holsom truck's just pulled outta Keasler's so the bread'll be like you like it. You sure you're not scared?"

"I don't know if I can," I lie.

"You know, sometimes you make me so mad I'd like to beat the stuffing outta you."

"Yeah, I'm *real* scared of that, Allie Rae."

"Well, well, well. Little Miss Mouse Fart's coming right along," she says, and slams down the phone.

I think it over and decide I'd better try to get down there. By the time I go ask Mama, she is on the phone. "Are you sure?" she asks, frown lines between her eyes. "Well, if you do see him, tell him to get himself home." Mama hangs up and rests her head in her hands.

Oh, no, Mama is hot on Daddy's trail. "Mama, Allie Rae's invited me to sleep over tonight. In the funeral home."

"What?" Mama doesn't even ask if Willie's going to be home or nothing. Just says, "Fine, be sweet." Great. So I can't use her as an excuse. I throw a nightshirt into a paper sack and head for Cedar Barton's.

Arriving at the stairwell leading up to Allie Rae's, I hesitate a minute. A chill blows off the tea-colored moon. The stairway going to the second floor is dim; a bald lightbulb dangles from a cord.

I hear Allie Rae banging pans and singing for all she's worth. She considers herself musically inclined.

"Is that you?" I call.

"Course it's me. Who were you expecting? A ghost perhaps?" She shrieks a hooting sound and waves her arms over the baloneyburger ingredients. She has on rhinestone sunglasses shaped like cat eyes, and a toothpick hangs from her lips.

"Stop hooting, Allie Rae. It's not funny."

"You know, you're so prissy, someday someone's just going to beat the stuffing outta you."

I am the least prissy person I know! "That's *not* true, but you say it all the time. What d'you mean?"

"It's cussing. Yep, cussing in disguise."

"Cussing?" I sputter. "Cussing?"

"Think about it for a minute. Here we are getting ready to eat baloneyburgers and then what? Well, a little bit of them will turn into us, and a great big pile'll be stuffing. And we all know what that turns into." She waits a healthy pause for effect. Allie Rae considers herself a great thinker. "Besides which, it saves on the S-word, and you never get in trouble."

I'm thinking I wish she knew how to save on the N-word when she begins frying baloney. Thick slices of onion and tomato line the counter, and the tomato bleeds thinly down the cabinet fronts. The baloney dances in the skillet and begins to pucker. "It's almost done when it curls up like that," Allie Rae says. "Look at it go."

We layer the baloneyburgers thick and pull chairs over by the window to eat. Then, as casually as if Allie Rae's inquiring about homework, she asks, "You ever sleep in a casket?" She sets her jelly glass down and looks straight at me.

A chill goosebumps my arm. Forget Mama and Bubba's old politeness rules. I've got to think of a good excuse to get myself outta here.

Allie Rae marches into her bedroom. She rolls

back her bed and tugs at the partition leading into the funeral home.

It sticks.

"Well, that's that," I say. When I prayed for a little excitement in my life, I did *not* have this in mind.

"The First Dead Person I Ever Saw"

Allie Rae pulls and pushes, and the partition creaks
open. She steps smartly into the casket room. Her
eyes dare me to follow. My heart's nearly jumping
out of my chest.

"A truckload just came in today," she reports
grandly, "all the way from Ohio. Yankee caskets and
I haven't even seen some of them yet. New models,
I betcha."

The smell of chemicals assaults me. Allie Rae
lights a match, and I see casket lids opened to the
same angle. They look like tombstones facing east,
waiting for Judgment.

"Now here's the important part," she says. "You've
got to take off your shoes. If Carlton finds out I've
been in these caskets again, he'll kill me. The last time
he smelled the matches, he asked Willie if I'd taken up
smoking. Willie told him it was her, but Willie says
I should be more careful because Carlton is wise to
what I'm doing. Now, take off your shoes."

"Allie Rae," I say, "if it's the same to you, I'm
awful tired. I'd like to save the caskets for later." I
can feel her eyes on me in the darkness like portraits
that stare back.

"So what've you got that's better?" she challenges.

The only sound is the clock, echoing through the casket room. It ticks and echoes and ticks some more.

"Well," I say, thinking hard, "my family knows lots of gory stuff too, collects it. We have a story about a man cut in two on the railroad tracks back of Keasler's. But I've got to be lying down in a regular bed to tell it because this story takes a lot outta you."

"Yeah?" says Allie Rae, getting interested and putting on her shoes and repositioning the partition.

We climb on her bed, and I start talking in a low, mysterious voice. "Now, remember, all of this happened a long time ago. A man named John Wesley Turner lived out on the Turkey Creek road, and he had a clubfoot, a wife, and about ten or eight kids. They were poor as gully dirt, but Mr. John Wesley walked to town two or three times a week selling eggs and vegetables and buying dry goods. One day, just after noon, the twelve o'clock train caught him on the tracks." By this time, my voice is shaking so bad I have trouble with mysterious, but I finally pull myself together and start up again. "Nobody could figure out why. Some said he was drinking; some said he was thinking. Anyways, the noontime train ran over him and cut him in two parts. Old Patterson was sitting out under the hickernut tree, and he actually saw the whole thing."

"You mean that cloudy-eyed old nig who sits by the tracks ever'day waving at the trains?"

"Colored. That's him. Colored. He saw everything, but even people who weren't there remember it like it happened yesterday. Why, I wasn't due to be born for years yet, and I consider Mr. John Wesley Turner the first dead person I ever saw," I say, stretching it out.

"Go on, go on," Allie Rae begs.

"Half of Mr. John Wesley lay on one side of the rail and half lay on the other, but his parts were connected by a pulsating, purple vein. His clubfoot twitched like a crow darting back and forth, waiting for rain. Bits of corn and peas he'd had for dinner scattered with the gravel along the tracks."

Allie Rae bolts straight up. "Oh, God, stuffing."

"His insides lay there for everyone to see. Old Dr. Jenkins came running up, but he just shook his head. Mr. John Wesley lived to say, 'Tell my brother to take care of my family.' He said it with his eyes sinking distant and becoming blind as a corpse's. His breath grew softer, and that was it."

Allie Rae moans, "That was *it*? Nobody picked him up? Where was Mr. Tom?"

"I *said* it was a long time ago. It was before the funeral home or the ambulance or Mr. Tom. Before all that. Back then, my great-grandmother Bom died at home in that folding oak bed we've got. They laid her out in the bedroom. Embalmed her *in Bubba's house*. They put her body under in the graveyard next to Papa's, but Bom's insides are buried somewheres in the chicken yard."

"At your grandmother's?" She whooshes air through her lips. "That's something," Allie Rae says. "It surely is, but this is worse somehow. Nothing else happened?"

"If it'll set your mind to rest, Dr. Jenkins got out his buggy and went a-runnin' to Turkey Creek and told Mr. John Wesley's brother, I guess. The End."

The room gets quiet for a while, then the night train rumbles through town. Allie Rae jerks a few times, the way people do in church trying to stay awake, and she makes a gentle noise in her nose. I lie wide-eyed waiting for morning, wondering if the dead get restless at night, shimmer up stairs like mist at sunrise.

The next thing I know, I wake up in pitch black, alone. I pat Allie Rae's side of the bed to make sure.

Except for me this bed is empty!

Immediately, I think of all those people who got a used casket that Allie Rae'd messed up, trying it out. What better time for those angry ghosts to get revenge than when the funeral home's nearly deserted?

They took Allie Rae first. Now they'll come back for me.

Jesus, please forget the dead a sec and help me, the living. I promise to do anything to pay you back. Become secretary for Methodist Youth Fellowship. Collect for those hungry missionaries in Africa. Quit looking at myself under the covers with a mirror.

The wind blows and I think I hear voices drifting

in and out. Probably the ghosts hooting and telling Allie Rae her time on earth is nearly up. Mine too.

Hurry it up, Jesus. I'll mend my ways, I promise, if you just . . .

"This Looks Big"

I start to cry, big time.

"What's the matter with you in there? Be quiet,"
Allie Rae hisses from the front room. "C'mere. Don't
know what's happening, but it's something big. Never
been like this before."

I fly in there, snuffling. "I've never been so scared
in all my life, Allie Rae. I thought ghosts got you for
sure, and were coming back for me."

"Get a hold of yourself," Allie Rae says. "Try to
think like other people for a change. *What* ghosts?"

Allie Rae has pulled the tweedy divan up to the
window and cracked the curtain. A shaft of light
profiles her. She has her knees drawn up, and her
chin rests on them. I move to the window. Down
below, people crowd the sidewalk in front of the
funeral home. Several cars, a pickup, and the ambulance are angle parked to the curb. The ambulance's
headlights beam a path into the darkness.

"Would you look at that?" Allie Rae says, and
sucks air through her teeth. "The law's there, and
Buckrod he dudn't get up for nothing past ten o'clock.
This looks big."

My eyes adjust to the darkness, and I see Sheriff

Buckrod in his khaki uniform with the star pinned over his heart. He swaggers to the back of the ambulance.

"You stay right here," Allie Rae says. "I'll see what's going on." She pulls a shirt over her night-gown and bounds downstairs. The clock on the end table ticks away, and its luminescent face reads three o'clock. I watch for what seems like hours, but when I look at the clock again, it says three thirty.

Allie Rae bursts back through the door, breathing hard, and gives an airy pat to her chest. "It's big, all right. Really big. You know that little lawyer down the street? The skinny, high-rumpted one with pointy collars?"

"Mr. Jud? Mr. Jud Sampson?"

"That's the one. That *was* him." She goes into one of her pauses. "Seems like, last night he drove his car out that road south of town. You know the one goes by Vance's farm?"

"Out near Black Mike's?"

"Yeah, that's right. Mr. Jud went on down the lane to the creek. Parked facing west, motor running." She purses her lips.

"Did anything in particular happen?" I ask in my most sarcastic voice.

"You bet. When Mr. Jud didn't come home by midnight, Miz Sampson she called up Buckrod, and he's the one who found Mr. Jud in his car with his brains splattered all over Cass County. Outta gas too."

"You mean . . ."

"Dead as he'll ever be, Silvy. Zilch. Here's the thing. I overheard Buckrod whispering to Mr. Drugstore Williams. He said it's most likely suicide."

"That'll break Miz Sampson's heart."

"I think it needs looking into," she announces like Nancy Drew, girl detective. "Most likely, Silvy, think. Who lives out those dark country roads? Lots and lots of darkies. Maybe one of 'em had a grudge against Mr. Jud."

How could she think that? I see Mr. Jud singing in the choir, going to school-board meetings, speaking to youth groups on Career Day. "Bad things like that don't happen here. Nobody would do such a thing."

"People like Mr. Jud have money, nice cars, everything. They don't need to take themselves to glory," Allie Rae says. "Still, if it got out that a nig was running around shotgunning white citizens, imagine the trouble. So Buckrod says 'most likely suicide,' pure and simple."

"Allie Rae, everybody liked Mr. Jud. He helped the poor, worked on committees, followed the law to a tee."

"He'll be law abiding from his grave, here on out. They're bringing him in now."

"Here?"

"Of course, here. Now don't start." She resettles

herself at the curtain and watches like it's a picture show.

For the first time, I'm a little nervous about my town and the people in it. What if she's right? What do I really know about the truth? I sit as close to Allie Rae as I can get, not ever wanting to be alone in a funeral home again.

"I Know Where Some Great Insides Are Buried"

~

By morning, I call Mama and say I want to come home. She pulls up to the funeral home with her hair still in bobby pins. "Silvy, honey, you okay?"

"It was awful, Mama, being there. A body came in. Mr. Jud's, Mama. Did you hear?"

"Listen, Silvy. Sad, unexplainable things happen. Your Daddy says the least we talk about it the better off for everyone. We have to think how Mr. Jud's death will affect poor Miz Sampson. She's always been one step ahead of a breakdown, and now this."

"It's so scary though. One day you're walking around, the next day you're laid out in Cedar Barton's."

"Don't think like that," Mama says, wringing her hands. "What was I thinking to let you sleep over at that funeral home?"

We drive home and Kingdom Hill never looked so good. Mama starts making her sour-cream pound cake to take to Miz Sampson, and I feed Sam Hill, go to bed, and sleep through the day and night.

Then Mama is shaking my shoulder, saying, "It's Sunday, churchtime. Wake up."

At church, the crowd's overflowing.

We go to our pew, seventh from the front on the right. Mim-Mim joins us and whispers, "Where's Allie Rae? This is the kind of thing she loves."

Allie Rae isn't here. She must be exhausted to miss a day like today.

When she isn't at school on Monday, I go looking.

At the funeral home, flowers cascade onto the sidewalk. But no Allie Rae; nobody's home.

I see Carlton and wonder if Mr. Jud will be getting a casket Allie Rae tried out or if he'll be getting a fresh one. Carlton says for me to run along on home, he doesn't know where Allie Rae is. Heading through Spring Park, I hear her voice coming from far away.

"Up here," she calls, as if from a tunnel.

She's perched in the top of the sycamore, and she doesn't look like herself. Her shoulders droop and her face looks vacant. She's holding on to the tree with one arm and staring out over the town.

"I've been looking all over for you," I yell up.

Her voice sounds flat and echoey. "C'mon up."

My knees tremble by the time I reach the top. "This is halfway to heaven."

"Did you happen to see Mr. Jud Sampson himself on your way up?" she asks in that hollow voice.

"Allie Rae, what's the matter?"

She starts crying in snuffles louder than her singing voice. Tears shine her upper lip. "I'm kicked outta school," she caterwauls. "Called on the carpet for talk."

"*What?*"

"Yep, Mr. Parsons phoned Willie yesterday and told her to keep me home till after the funeral."

"Why?" I ask, thinking I haven't heard right.

"Well," Allie Rae says, "it seems like in this hick town, you don't talk about the well-to-do dead. At least, not their parts, brains, and stuff. Parsons told Willie it'd be disrespectful if I came back knowing what I know about Mr. Sampson. Guess that means I'm not good enough for all y'all."

"That's not true, Allie Rae."

"How'd you like it if you always smelled like stale flowers? I hate living where everyone talks like a country-western singer, and nobody says what they think. No bowling alleys or libraries, a bummed-out picture show. Stupid teachers and nosy old widow women. For excitement, we can always go to Miss Maggie's recital or dinner on the grounds after church. How can you stand it?"

"It's not *so* bad," I say feebly. But I'm beginning to think maybe it is.

"Huh! You have no idea what it's like for me," she says with a look. "Even you, Silvy."

That is so hurtful it's disgusting. I'm the one who tries to stand up for her. "What's that mean?"

"It's not enough that you live in a sappy house, but you know who both your parents are. You know your grandparents and all their particulars. You even know who your great-grandparents were, and you're still carrying on about where their *insides* are buried."

She cups her hands to her mouth. "Hey, down there," she yells in hiccuppy sobs, "if anybody's interested, I know where some *great* insides are buried."

A sour taste rises in my throat. She's right. I do talk about my people a lot when she's only got a mama.

"Allie Rae, fact is, I don't know who my grandfather is. He's just the Missing Man to me. Kinda like your daddy. And I don't know where Bom's insides are either, exactly. When I was little, I used to be afraid to play near the barn. I didn't want to step on no ghosts. It's not a big thing."

Allie Rae sniffs and wipes a stream of snot on her hand. "Easy for you to say. Old Parsons told Willie I'd be better off not knowing so much. He said I added a 'chatty dimension' to the classroom. Said I had friends, but he'd noticed I only had friends at school. Even that old fart knows people are afraid to visit me. Can Mim-Mim sleep over? No! And there I was all the time thinking I'm the perfect hostess. Frying up baloneyburgers. I should've just gone to the door and said, 'What would you like dear, something in oak with soft satin lining?'"

"Please stop, Allie Rae."

"Everyone's gotta die, so what's the big deal? Ride more trees. Life's a party," she says, honks like a donkey, and then clams up.

This is scary. I've never seen Allie Rae afraid of

anything. But here she is, crying, thinking she isn't worth nothing 'cause her mama's not married normal-like and she lives in the wrong place. Maybe she's crying 'cause she really believes a murderer's on the loose.

I'm trapped in a town where you better toe the line. Otherwise you could end up miserable as Allie Rae. You could end up wondering about everything.

I need to distract her. Looking through the leaves, I can barely make out Miss Clara and Miss Hattie, "the girls from Maiden Lane," sitting on their bench. "Don't want to cheer you too much, but this must be your lucky day. I see your guardian angels."

It gets so quiet in that tree you'd think it's Sunday. Allie Rae looks down at the park. Then she says a very bad word, the stuffing word. Miss Clara and Miss Hattie are sitting on their scrawny rumps with their barrel chests resting on their stomachs, their skinny legs dangling over twig-like ankles. They look at us with noses in the air.

"You'd think they'd like tree climbing," I say. "Back when they were young, it must've been fashionable. A necessity of sorts."

To my relief, Allie Rae nudges my foot in a sort of apology. She turns her red-edged eyes my way and says, "Why?"

"Back then, they were still living in the treetops."

She cracks a smile and sets off swinging. As I

hug the tree, she starts the swaying. We dip into a frisky wind and then shoot upward.

"To hell with 'em both," she says, and her spirits begin to rise like sap.

I'm Thinking Not Enough Said

Two weeks before Halloween, Mama needs a favor. She says, sugar-voiced, "Silvy, honey, since you're too old to go out this year, would you take Larry and Sara trick-or-treating? Maybe help with their costumes?"

Too old? "Sure thing, Mama," I agree, figuring it's the only way I'll get to go. Sara wants to be a nurse, I decide to go as a Gypsy with jewelry made of canning-jar rings, and Larry changes his mind about a million times. Finally, he sets his heart on being the pirate Trammel.

"Listen here, Silvy," he bosses, "I want shiny purple pants, a shirt with puffy sleeves, an eye patch, and a sword. Got that? The rest will be up to me."

Who does my brother think he is? But Bubba tells me to try her brother Hank, my great-uncle, who once was an Aggie at A&M University and pranced around in fancy clothes. "How those Aggies carried on at ball games," she laughs.

After school Monday, I catch up with Uncle Hank in his little apartment over Keasler's. He's wearing a green plastic eye visor and carrying a ledger in his big, square hands. "How's my sweet niece?" he asks, his blue eyes crinkling.

"Good as can be, Uncle Hank. We're working on costumes, and Larry wants to be Trammel for trick-or-treating, so we need shiny pants, a sash, and a shirt with big sleeves. Bubba says you wore fancy Aggie clothes."

"I see," he chuckles. "Why use old musty stuff? Let's go down and find new material for the fierce Trammel."

In dry goods, Uncle Hank dismisses the clerk. "I'll take care of this customer myself." Without even measuring, he cuts purple satin for Larry's pants and a yellow cotton strip for his sash, then he rummages through piles of shirts before finding one with big sleeves. He never once looks at a price tag. "That should do it," he says to the clerk, who's hung around watching as though this is the way to do business.

"Almost, Uncle Hank. Larry wants a sword."

"Have just the thing, Silvy, but we need to go back to my apartment."

Up there, Uncle Hank moves some books off a dusty trunk. In our family, Uncle Hank's the best talker. "Uncle Hank, you knew my grandfather, didn't you?"

He turns slowly toward me. "Now what brought that up?"

Truth is, Allie Rae got me thinking about family

things. "I've always wanted to know what he was like."

Uncle Hank rests on his heels. "Let me say that he was quite a fellow; he liked a good time. He and your grandmother spent hours, sometimes from dawn till dark-thirty, walking Trammel's Trace, collecting wildflowers, and quoting poetry. He was different."

"You telling me he was a Yankee?"

"Some folks think anyone who's not a Texan is a Yankee. He was just one of those fellas who looked at things in a different way. 'Nuff said."

But I'm thinking, not enough said!! Why is the Missing Man missing? What happened, anyways?

Without another word, Uncle Hank resumes digging through the trunk. At the bottom, he finds his A&M sword. He raises the sword reverently and sings in his cheery voice: "The eyes of Texas are upon you, that is the song they sing so well. So good-bye to Texas University. We're gonna beat you all to—"

Uncle J. D. barges in. "How many times do I have to tell you, Hank? We won't make a thin dime giving merchandise away. Especially to, uh . . . family."

Grabbing material, I start for the door. Leaving, I hear Uncle J. D. and Uncle Hank get into an argument everyone can hear all the way through groceries. When I tell Mama what happened, her eyes narrow, and mid-story, she cuts me off. "What do you *mean,* begging?"

"I wasn't! Uncle J. D. caused it all. It's him with his ugly manners."

"Do not bad-mouth your uncle. He seems severe at times, but Uncle J. D. looks out for our interests. Our bills are sometimes a little overdue, so watch it."

"Y'all Are Good, but I Knew You Right Off"

Mama's sticking up for Uncle J. D. takes some fun out of getting our costumes ready, but not all of it. On Halloween, we start down Kingdom Hill. It's moonless and windy, gobliny and ghosty, a perfect night for trick-or-treating.

We stop at the foot of the hill where Miss Blue, our closest neighbor, lives. She's waiting on her porch, a bowl of peanuts in her lap, a candle setting the scene. "Evening, Miss Blue," Larry says.

"Looky who's here," she cackles.

After commenting how we almost scared her to death, Miss Blue hands us each three counted-out raw peanuts. As we're leaving, she hollers, "Y'all are good, but I knew you right off. You should of seen the ones before you. Never saw such realistic little jigs."

Somebody's costumed as the coloreds? That seems downright tacky.

We meet lots of kids and get the usual: popcorn balls, caramel apples, candy. At practically every house, they mention the tricksters in front of us. "Cutest kids ever. You never saw such antics."

Up ahead, I see two girls I don't recognize. They

must be the ones everyone mentioned. We drop back and follow them. They're having the best time, laughing and slapsticking. One does most of the talking, and the way she skips along she seems like a real ghost, almost floating. The other girl looks around every few steps.

Sure enough, they're dressed like coloreds, pigtails on the talky one, bandanna on the other. Going from house to house, they sound pretty normal, but when someone comes to the door, they way overdo. Too many "Yaz-ums," too much bowing.

They head toward Bubba's. "Old Missus's house," I hear.

Larry gets on his high horse. "Did you hear that girl call Bubba old?"

I heard. "Let's sneak into these camellia bushes and watch."

The talky girl pounds on Bubba's screen door like she's intending to break it. She explains to her friend, "Those big flowerpots in there, 'urns' they calls 'em, belonged to Miss Bom before most of her went to Jesus. Her insides are buried out in that chicken yard. Who-eee."

I get it suddenly, how much she knows and how she skims along.

Bubba finally comes to the door. "Well, looky who's here," she says, leaning into the screen, shading her eyes. "Oh! My goodness, how cute. Who is it?" Bubba begins guessing.

"Naw."

"Naw."

"Naw."

Guessed out, Bubba asks outright, "Okay, so tell."

"It's the coloreds!"

"T'isn't," Bubba says, "but I have to admit, you could have fooled me. Your makeup is good. Now 'fess up."

"No'um," they say together, like a duet.

"Guess I'll just have to find out later in the *New Era*," Bubba concedes.

"Guess so," says the big talker. They take their Hershey bars and head into the night, leaving Bubba wondering. "Scared me a little at first, but they are really clever. Cutest little things. Wish all coloreds were like them, they'd never cause trouble."

Those two have lots of nerve! Coloreds exaggerating the coloreds. But why? It's dangerous. I check that no one's around before yelling, "Hey, Mabelee, *trick*-or-*treat!*"

They stop as if lassoed, then Mabelee's friend takes off like a turpentined dog. Mabelee plants her feet and confronts us. Her face is jet black, and she has lipsticked huge red lips around her mouth. She looks scared.

"Would you hush up, Silvy? Can't imagine what'll happen if we get caught."

Me neither. Everyone knows that coloreds are supposed to be off the streets by night, even kids.

It's a law no one ever breaks. Daddy says cross burn-
ings and lynchings once happened around here for
things like this.

"How'd you know?" Mabelee challenges.

I've known her since she almost wasn't. "I don't
see how you could think I wouldn't know you,
Mabelee."

"We blacked our faces with soot. You ever see
anybody this colored before? No! Fooled everybody,
even your grandmother."

"*Old* Missus," Larry says disgustedly.

"Just mouthing off," Mabelee admits, "but everyone thought we were so cute. Mr. Drugstore Williams
gave us nickels like we could spend them at his soda
counter. Old Miss Blue asked did I want to set a spell.
Now that'd be something, huh? Me setting out there
with that old white woman eating three goober peas."

I grab her by the elbows. "Mabelee, you're taking
a chance being over here at night. You know that.
So, why?"

"I tell you why. I was wondering what it's like
being white, Silvy. Go into Keasler's, tee in the toilet.
Go to the City Drug, have a red pop, fine as you
please, or just get me a drink at the fountain . . ."

"Oh, Mabelee," I say, not knowing how to
continue.

"You ever read Mr. Paul Laurence Dunbar's
poetry? Probably not, 'cause he's colored. He
wrote one about masks, tells just how I feel. You

should read it sometime. He's as good as your old Shakespeare any day."

I'm shocked. 'Course I haven't heard of a colored poet.

"Well, you know what?" she says, as if announcing a great discovery. "It ain't as good as I was thinking being over here for Halloween. Too many scary white faces out to get you." She looks at me like I'm one of 'em.

I want to tell her to be careful, watch out, but I don't.

Leaving, she has the last say: "Canning rings in your ears is strange, Silvy, but I guess you did the best you could with what you got. Still, you being a Gypsy, you won't be sunburning. Funny, huh? You dark too. Trick-or-treat!"

Mabelee turns, ribboned head high, and disappears into the night that gobbled her friend. Looks like someone is teaching her some powerful lessons.

I grab Larry and Sara by their shoulders. "Listen up. Do not ever, *ever*, in a zillion years mention this. To anybody." I give them a little shake. "It could be dangerous for them. Got it?"

"For us too," Larry mumbles, and Sara nods, her eyes wide as someone being strangled.

The next few days, and then weeks, everyone keeps wondering about the "colored" trick-or-treaters.

Someone suggests maybe it was even two of *them*!

"Sacrilege!"

The talk keeps buzzing though it's almost Thanksgiving. Walking to the drugstore for a Coke, Allie Rae wonders, "It's a complete mystery why those colored trick or treaters didn't claim first-prize money, huh?"

I don't mention what I'm wondering.

The City Drug is a long brick building with rusty awnings facing Main Street. Blindfolded, you'd know where you were from the smells: old bricks, vanilla, menthol, stale cigarette smoke, and perfume. Mr. Williams, the pharmacist, meets us at the door. "Hidy, girls. Ready to start thinking about Christmas?"

Allie Rae eyes him sideways. "Pretty much," she says. Allie Rae does not trust pharmacists. Those people can kill you with the flick of a pill, she often advises, 'specially if they're prone to take a drink.

"Did you hear the town's having a Christmas parade?" Mr. Williams asks. "Lions Club is working on it now."

"*Really?*" says Allie Rae, her eyes widening, and then to me, "Now, *that's* grand."

When I tell Mama about the parade, she wants the Methodist Youth Fellowship to enter a float.

"That's the craziest thing I ever heard, Mama. We have to study for tests before school lets out for Christmas. I can't be both smart and decorated."

Mama snaps, "I'll get a committee, you watch." She hasn't always been so snappish. Seems like the more money problems we have, the more fly-off-the-handle she gets. In her old voice she says, "Honey, let's start over. Why don't you tell me what you want for Christmas?"

"A bike and a guinea pig in a store-bought cage, a pump BB gun, and shiny, clicking tap-dancing shoes."

The minute I finish my list, I realize Bubba's behind me and I've made a mistake. Bubba peers over her glasses. "You know, Silvy, when I was a girl, I only got one orange for Christmas, and you top off with dancing shoes. Uh!"

How could my grandmother settle for an orange?

"Lots of perfectly normal, modern people dance nowdays, you know."

"Did Allie Rae tell you that?"

"Of course not, no, but what if she did?"

"I'll tell you what if she did, Sister. It's the devil's handiwork, dancing and game-playing for money. I'm glad Papa didn't live to see the day you'd be dancing a jig in Spring Park. Does Allie Rae go?"

Mama seems as interested in my answer as Bubba. "Sometimes," I mumble. "But she just watches. Mostly." It's an uncomfortable feeling when one of you is lying, and all of you know it.

"I'm right sorry to hear that," Bubba says, "but

what'd you expect? Can't blame the poor thing, living over a funeral parlor, doesn't have an idea in the world who her people are. She'll probably end up in a dance hall, and it won't be her fault, either," she finishes generously.

I stomp into my room.

Next morning, Mama starts calling MYFers to work on the float. Even Duane says no. Finally, Billy Mathison volunteers.

I tell Mama that Billy is a mistake. His idea of fun is starting grass fires. Sometimes he writes funny words in church-hymnal titles. After "I Have Found a Friend in Jesus," he'll scribble "Under the Bed." Or "The Old Rugged Cross Under the Bed." Mama should get somebody with brains, like James Barnes, the new kid, even though you can tell he's a Yankee. (Bubba says you never ask anyone where they're from. If they come from Texas, they'll tell you right off, and if not, no need to embarrass them.)

Mama doesn't think much of my advice. "As far as Billy goes," she says, "he's willing to help, and he has a good heart." Wonder what she'd say if she knew Billy only reads the dirty parts of the Bible? Getting him to do right is like herding cats.

Saturday afternoon Larry, Sara, and I go downtown to look at Christmas decorations. We don't have any money, but we drop by the City Drug anyways. Tub comes in and when he sees us, he sticks his hand in his pocket and jingles coins. Then he says, the way he always does, "My babies here gonna have themsefs a sody. If you ain't got a red 'un, they take a green 'un."

This makes me feel strange. Tub can't have a soda at the City Drug with us. He doesn't have much money, but here he's treating us.

Everything seems to hit me these days. I didn't use to notice. I'm hearing things now too. One night on the radio, a program told how the Supreme Court voted to let coloreds ride the buses—from one state to another. The announcer said that happened a few years back, but now they're sure to try it. He choked, "World War II put uprising in the air. Got them crying, 'Let 'em fight, let 'em ride.'" Then he added one day that same Court might let coloreds go wherever they wanted. I thought just *why not?* I can't see Jesus having separate places to sit at the Last Supper.

I said that to Bubba, and she cried, "Sacrilege!" Then she said I should watch it, I'm telling everything on my mind these days down to the wrinkles in my drawers.

Now I hear Tub say, "Thank you kindly," when the soda jerk puts three soda pops on the counter— red ones for Sara and me and a green one for Larry. Tub lifts his empty hand in an imaginary toast. "Many happy days," he says.

"To you too, Tub," I toast him, wondering if he'll ever know how much I mean it.

"The Whipped Cream on the Pie"

When Mim-Mim calls with news, her voice always sounds breathy. Today, she's positively winded. "You sitting down, Silvy? You won't be*lieve* this. Lester Fulton's teamed up with Billy to work on the MYF float."

Lester Fulton has a mess of mean-eyed brothers and sisters. They hang off their porch fighting each other, and they lay outta school whenever they feel like it. Still, they show up everywheres and are into everything. You'd expect to see an angel shelling peas quicker than an artistic Fulton. *"What?!"*

"It gets better. Lester wants to put worms on the float. Worms, Silvy," she gulps, "ordinary night crawlers. He says those moving worms will make it look like a gentle breeze's blowing over the manger and baby Jesus."

I try to warn Mama about the crisis fixing to happen, but she's not listening. "It's generous of Lester to make a donation," is what she says.

Eve was generous with the apple too, but look where that went. "Mama, you've got to do something."

"Stop it, Silvy," Mama says, way too loud for a mother-daughter conversation. "Your grandmother and I are trying to hold this family's finances together. I can't handle one more thing today. Worms or no worms makes me no nevermind."

Right now, I do not understand Mama, and Mama does not understand me.

Saturday dawns sparkly with icicles, perfect for the Christmas parade. Allie Rae and Mim-Mim bring cocoa, and we huddle together against the cold. The whole county has turned out, breaths rising like chimney smoke on Main Street.

Across the street where the coloreds stand, I spot Mabelee in a bright red jacket. She's stamping her feet and blowing into her hands. I give her a wave she doesn't see. I wave again, harder. This time she nods her head slightly. Allie Rae whispers, "You know what they call people who love 'em, don't you?" I tell her to hush up and she chuckles, "Heh, heh. Got-cha!"

The parade begins. The wind, about two puffs shy of a tornado, fairly howls "Jolly Old St. Nicholas" along with the band.

Allie Rae draws in her breath and points. "Look. Who's that darky? He's dressed fit to kill, huh?" Mim-Mim snaps to attention. "He's sure not one of ours, more like the whipped cream on the pie, I'd say."

A young colored man, dressed in a suit and tie, is smiling confidently, leaning on a lamppost. Mabelee rushes to his side. She's obviously glad to see him, laughing and gesturing the way she used to do with me. Moving through the coloreds, he and Brother Posey have sheets of paper, and every now and then someone signs something. Oh, Lordy—I look away. Was he smiling at me?

Why would he do that?

Allie Rae asks, "You suppose that darky is a friend of Brother Posey's?" I overlook her ugliness, but wonder myself. The young man's unusual for around here, that's certain, and it could spell trouble.

Next thing I know, the colored man's vanished. Now you see him, now you don't. Why didn't he stick around till the parade ended? Sheriff Buckrod moves through the crowd, his eyes scanning like search-lights, and then he crosses over to the coloreds' side.

Brother Posey lifts his hat to Buckrod, smiling. Buckrod shuffles through Brother Posey's papers, shakes his head, says something, and gives back the papers. Returning to our side of Main Street, he and Mr. Drugstore Williams have a long, head-shaking conversation. Mr. Williams tap-tap-taps Buckrod's star with his finger.

We spot the MYF float chugging down Main Street. Earlier today, the wiggling worms *did* look like a gentle wind blowing over that manger. But now, the harder the wind blows, the drier Lester's worms get. By the time the float reaches Keasler's, worms are blowing ever'whichway. It smells like a truckload of rotting lilies. "Gag a maggot," Allie Rae says, holding her nose.

The Baptist Training Union kids' float, a wobbly, open Bible made of Kleenex stuffed in chicken wire, wins. Mama's the only one surprised it beat the worm mobile.

"You Got Anything Needs Doing?"

On Monday, I head to town to shop for Bubba's
Christmas present. Passing Keasler's, I spot Mabelee
in the alley, having a red pop with some of her
friends. It's awkward after the parade. Should I go
over there? Our eyes meet, and she takes some steps.
We meet halfway.

"Hey," she greets me, sounding a little muffled.
Then she slaps her knees and hoots, "Us colored
MYFers could've done better in that parade, Silvy.
Y'all's float looked like a Bible plague. Bethlehem
wasn't exactly known for worms, you know." She's
tickling herself to death.

"You're absolutely right, girl," I admit. Then talking gets strained. "So how's ever'thing?" It sounds
feeble even to me.

She shrugs. "Um, 'bout the same. Town's town.
School's school. Except you won't believe what
they're doing out there. Brother Posey got some of
his army buddies together, and they've painted up
our schoolhouse right pretty."

"Sounds good. Did it need it?"

"*Need* it? You kidding me, Silvy? The last time
that building saw paint, Mama was a baby. Brother

Posey says we got to make things better our ownself. I reckon he's right."

Brother Posey gets things done. He's a preacher you can't help but like. Even Allie Rae says it's a shame he's colored.

"So I'm going to be helping," Mabelee adds, a little chagrined now. "Me and my girlfriends, we going to earn money for new books. You got anything needs doing? Anything 'cept walking that goat?" She smiles. I don't.

This makes me so uncomfortable. Do *I* have anything that needs doing? The employer and the servant . . . the master and the slave. Near'bout speechless, I stammer, "I'll, I'll let you know, Mabelee."

"Sure," she says with a look that shows she doesn't know me nomore either.

I duck into the City Drug to shop for Bubba's gift. She doesn't like fashion so perfume's out. Bath powders won't do 'cause they make her sneeze. Vitamins aren't much of a gift either. Anyways, I want something special, a gift she'll remember.

I give up shopping and begin the lonely walk toward Kingdom Hill. Mabelee's request for work plays like a record in my head.

At home, Christmas has jumped the fence. Our house smells like pine and cookies. But nothing under our tree says me! Nothing's hidden either. I've looked everywhere.

One night when Mama and Daddy are arguing in the kitchen, they start out loud with "dominoes" mentioned a bunch. "You've got to pay something on our grocery bill," Mama says. "It's never been this high."

"You mean spend our gift money for groceries?" Daddy asks incredulously.

Mama drums her fingers on the kitchen table. "Watch it, 'Ears' may be listening." It usually burns me up when Mama calls me that. But this close to Christmas, she may have meant it in a nice way, to protect surprises.

If there are any.

Christmas morning, Sara wakes up everybody screaming, "Santy Claus! Santy Claus!" I drag into the living room, not expecting much, but hoping just the same.

Larry gets the BB gun, a Red Ryder propped under the tree, and Sara is hugging a blonde-headed walking doll. As the doll steps smartly around the tree, I spot shiny dancing shoes beneath a decorated branch.

Seeing Daddy's face, I know *he* got those shoes for me. Must've hidden them in his truck. Feeling like the luckiest girl alive, I twirl around the tree.

When Bubba sees my gift, she doesn't say one bad word about dancing. Maybe because it's Christmas. Mama and Daddy like the mashed-elf story I wrote them. Daddy says, "Who'd ever think an elf could get himself in a fix like that?"

Bubba starts unwrapping her present from me. She tears off the paper, lifts the lid, and does a double take. I may be in a fix myself. Bubba leans into the box and takes a big sniff like it's perfume from the City Drug. I hold my breath. "Oh, Silvy," she says, her eyes glistening, "I've never gotten a better gift." She throws back her head and holds up the orange.

Yep, I figure this is the best family anywheres, Missing Man and all. My good-Christmas feelings have me almost tasting the black-eyed peas we'll eat for New Year's good luck, the fireworks we'll shoot celebrating 1954's arrival.

Then on the last day of the year I run up Kingdom Hill—and Sam Hill has disappeared.

"Not a Matter of Wrong, Exactly"

Sam Hill's not missing, he's *gone!* His chain's not on the stake, and only his smell is left.

"Where in hell is Sam Hill?" I shout, copying Daddy. When Mama doesn't wash out my mouth with soap, I know he's gone forever. She looks away, sad. "He had to go."

"Where?"

"Let's just say he went to a new home. Girls shouldn't learn their manners from goats, and your daddy can't spend his time rounding up Sam Hill. So don't make him feel any worse than he does."

They're in this together! (When Mama says "your father," it's him; when she says "your daddy," it's them.) If I had magic powers, I'd turn them both into their own bad dreams. Daddy'd be a sorry domino player, and Mama'd be a Baptist. "Neither of you cares a donkey's patoot how I feel. Why couldn't I have been born on a ranch with nice parents?"

I dream about those parents sometimes: fashionable Stetson hats, matching fringed outfits, cowboy boots. They provide a proper barn for my goat and accompany me to horse shows to pick up gold trophies. Cheering wildly.

"I hate you," I wind up.

"Go to your room," Mama says, her voice quivering. "And stay there until you get yourself composed."

I stay through New Year's Day. Let 1954 happen without me. Larry slides the *New Era* under my door, but it just has articles on car crashes, a house fire, and something about "unrest" in the bottom, doesn't say who or what. Only "unrest."

While I'm getting myself composed, I vow I'll never be the white-on-white, sweet-smelling, boring girl my parents want, no matter what.

When I think I might starve, I put on clean clothes and go into the kitchen. Larry and Sara stare at me, big-eyed; I've never missed a meal before. "Morning," Mama says gently, frying bacon. "I want you to know I'm sorry about Sam Hill, but sometimes you do what you must. I hope you're feeling better."

I'm not.

After breakfast, I go looking for Allie Rae and find her in Spring Park, reading a fingernail-polish label. Products fascinate her. She spends hours wondering how much salt the little Morton girl spilled, why Bon Ami hasn't scratched yet, or what makes red pop red. "Where you been?" she asks. "Thought you hibernated."

"Allie Rae, Sam Hill's disappeared—two days ago. I'm goatless." I burst into tears.

"For Pete's sake," Allie Rae says, "don't be so gloomy. That creature stunk and his stench came

off on you sometimes. You can have better company
with a little social effort."

How can she be so heartless? She lowers her voice
chummily and nods toward the street. "Looking at
her makes me sick."

Kathy Bryers, a girl our age, is limping clink, clink,
slide toward the park. She's dressed out of fashion
in a long dress to hide her braces, and she moves so
slowly it doesn't look like she'll make it up a slight
incline.

"Don't say that, Allie Rae!" I gasp. "She can't help
it. She had that bulbar stuff, worst kind of polio, and
she was in an iron lung forever. They had to burn all
her toys and clothes."

"I didn't *say* she could help being a cripple, Silvy.
If you look like that, you should have sense enough
to stay home, that's all." No response tops a remark
that ugly. Next Allie Rae gives a low whistle. "Uh-
oh, look again."

The young colored man from the parade walks up
to Kathy and offers his arm to help her on the incline. I can't believe what I'm seeing. Broad daylight:
white girl, colored man, together in the park. Puts
me to shame. I didn't even help Mabelee raise money
for her school, and here he's helping a stranger, a
white stranger.

"That's so disgusting. Two cripples, you ask me,"
Allie Rae says. "Could cause big trouble if they hit
Main Street."

She's right, I know, but today I'm sick of her. Allie Rae doesn't have sympathy for anybody—goats, cripples, or coloreds.

The colored man walks on as if nothing happened. I decide to get myself going too. "See you later. I've got an errand."

Puzzled, she scowls, "Sure thing," and I hightail it home where I feel sorry for myself, good and proper. My parents don't understand me, I live in a town that's stupid and scary, and someone's got my goat.

Duane, on the other hand, has got himself a fabulous new horse, Ike, who can rear up on his hind legs and jump gullies like an expert. Just as I'm picturing myself riding Ike and becoming part of the wind, Bubba's car pulls up. "Sister, come here," she calls, and I do, but I take my sweet time. "Yes Ma'am?"

"Your mama and I've been talking. We think you need to take a few lessons over at Maggie's."

"Why?" I explode. "What am I doing wrong?"

"Wh-oa," Bubba stammers, "it's not a matter of 'wrong' exactly. This time anyway," she admits, holding up her hands as if pleading with the windshield. "You need a little instruction, some talent development, something to get your mind off, well, other things. And this playing just the white keys on the piano is frankly pathetic. So your mama and I, with your daddy being all for it too I must add, have decided that you will take a few music lessons at Maggie's. Nothing spectacular. We will personally handle your how-to-do lessons, and you won't have to worry about that part a'tall." She ends up gasping for breath.

A few piano lessons won't be half as bad as the School of Manners. "Bubba, I appreciate it."

"You *do?*" She climbs out of her car and grabs my hand, shaking it. "Your poor mama thought you'd resist."

"No Ma'am, I'm grateful. I was just thinking this very minute about how I have everything I need"— Bubba nods in agreement—"except a horse."

"I knew it," Bubba says, straightening up to her full six-feet height. She glares icicles. "Good try, but nothing doing. You're too reckless, Silvy. You'd damage your womanly insides."

Here I've been praying out my eyes for boobs, and she's moved on to my womanly insides. "Well, Ma'am, if I can't have a horse, I was just thinking . . ."

"Don't overdo the 'ma'am.' Just state your case."

"I was kinda wondering if Mabelee could come when you and Mama teach me how-to-do?"

"The very idea," Bubba says softly. Then she exclaims, "My stars!"

"You know you and Mama don't really think Mabelee has good manners, do you?"

"Let's-s-s, uh, just say she has a different kind of manners." Bubba begins sounding like a diamond-back.

"Then let's teach her ours. You always say she's a nice girl, just a little loud."

"True," Bubba nods, working up some enthusiasm.

"It wouldn't hurt anything. Yes, indeedy. I've always liked Mabelee. If you'll practice real hard on the piano, I think your mama will agree to Mabelee's coming."

Home run! Mabelee will make how-to-do fun.

We Wear the Mask

One Saturday in early spring, Mabelee comes to Kingdom Hill for how-to-do. I am so happy I'm singing. Then I suddenly wonder if she's only coming so she can try to raise money for their school. But she greets me loudly, and everything seems pretty much okay.

After hanging up her coat, she hums a zippy tune. Mama and Bubba are readying-up in the kitchen, and I'm itching to find out some stuff. "Mabelee, I saw this colored man with Brother Posey at the Christmas parade. Walks straight as a bean stob and dresses fine. You know the one?"

"Reckon I might. Good-looking with gray striped pants and a white, itchy-looking shirt? Smart-talking too, like on the radio?"

"I couldn't hear what he said, but yeah, that sounds about right. Who is he? What brings him here?"

Mabelee clasps her hands. "Ain't he special? That's Obadiah's nephew, Jefferson. Studied how to build buildings up North. Architect. Came here for a visit when he couldn't get a job architecting. Can you imagine, knowing all that stuff, drawing all them buildings, and still no work, nowheres? Brother Posey's helping him out. Has him working as our church youth adviser."

So they got a youth adviser. "He nodded at me. Why?"

"I pointed you out, said we'd been friends from the get-go. He don't go to town much now 'cause Mr. Buckrod told him he don't want no stranger coming in and stirring up trouble. But that Jefferson, he's fine to look at, huh?"

I nod 'cause it's true. Wow! Colored men going to college and learning to design buildings. Colored youth adviser. Coloreds raising money and painting their own school. Change is looking 'round the corner. It's breathing down Buckrod's neck too. And he's noticed.

Mabelee starts whispering as if she knows the world's best secret. "Jefferson's got himself a radio, and he's ever'day listening to news. Says there's a colored man in Kansas, name of Oliver Brown, who wants his daughters to go to the white school. One of those kids, name of Linda, is about our age. Whoo-ee, is that causing a ruckus! Jefferson says the Supreme Court men heard Mr. Brown's case first time in 1952, but couldn't decide nothing. They thought on it again last December 1953, but they'll probably keep taking their own sweet time. Can you imagine us going to school together, Silvy?"

I surely, surely can't, though I'd heard this on

the radio myself. Mr. Brown's lawyers and members of the National Association for the Advancement of Colored People were arguing that keeping our schools apart—white and colored, "separate but equal"—was unconstitutional.

"Whoa, Mabelee. You think?" I whisper back. "Maybe someday in Kansas, but *here?*"

"You girls ready to get started?" Mama asks as she and Bubba come into the dining room for how-to-do.

"Yessum," Mabelee says.

Mama flinches. "Yes ma'am," she says, enunciating carefully, Bubba nodding like a metronome.

"Yes *ma'am,*" Mabelee mimics a teense too loud for polite. Mama and Bubba shoot each other looks, but they don't say anything.

Table settings are our first lesson: flower arrangements, linens, silverware placement. "Lah, lah, lah. Would you look at me," Mabelee warbles, making a lilac centerpiece for the table.

We move into the dining room where Mama shows how to drape the tablecloth evenly. "It's best to put the cloth on the night before and smooth the wrinkles with your hands," she explains.

"That right?" Mabelee says in a tone flatter than hoecakes.

Bubba starts setting the table. "We've laid it, now we set it," she says.

Mabelee wrinkles her whole face. "Missus, if you don't mind me saying so, three forks is two too many."

Well, Bubba tells Mabelee that she does, in fact, mind. She says some people have shrimp cocktails often.

"Not me," answers Mabelee with pluck. "I use one fork, and it works right fine."

After forks, Mabelee rubs her back. "Boyoboy, feels like I been ironing all day in my bare feet. No snuff, neither." She grins, but she's the only one grinning. Bubba looks defeated.

"Mabelee, you must try," Mama says kindly.

Mabelee says she's got to meet Goldie at Keasler's, and she puts on her coat. When she tells me goodbye, she whispers, "Why you want to know this old stuff? I'd rather be learning dance steps or drinking red pop or 'most anything."

Once again she's aced me. "I'd rather be doing other things myself, Mabelee." Still, a deal is a deal.

Before she leaves, she hands me a piece of paper. "I wrote out Mr. Dunbar's poem. You might want to read it sometimes." I glance at it, "We Wear the Mask," and stuff it in my pocket.

That night Mim-Mim calls and I'm telling her about our how-to-do lesson. She giggles. "What'd your grandmother do when Mabelee said that about the snuff?" she asks.

"Mabelee says what she's thinking, that's for sure. She's excited about this good-looking colored man, who—"

From his easy chair, Daddy asks in a not-so-easy

way, "Hang up that phone, Silvy. Did my ears hear right and a daughter of mine just called a colored boy 'good-looking'?"

"I didn't mean anything by it."

"I don't ever want to hear something like that come out of your mouth again, Silvy. You can't talk like that here. People might take it wrong."

"Yessir," I say, shaky voiced.

Daddy looks bewildered. "Things are changing, and change tends to get folks riled up. Even I got mad at Goldie last week when she asked if I wanted to buy a pie. I told her when I want one of her pies, I can step into Bubba's kitchen when she makes one. She looked so hurt, I felt bad. But changing how we do is a bunch of foolishness, you ask me. There's even talk about one day combining our schools. Not that it'll happen here, so don't you worry."

I'm not worried, just confused. Whatever happened to what we learn in Sunday school—be they yellow, black, or white, they are precious in His sight? "Did you know any colored soldiers, Daddy?"

Daddy folds the sports page. "Listen to me Silvy, please, it's important. Of course I knew some, and they were fine fellas for the most part. Fought and died same as anybody. But around here this colored-white issue is a different kind of war. People can get hurt, bad. So watch what you do and watch what you say. Got it?"

Now I am worried. "Yessir."

I've heard scary stuff before, but this is the first
time anybody's called it war! I shudder thinking about
what Daddy said, how troubled he looked, and that
night I start reading the poem Mabelee gave me.

We wear the mask that grins and lies,
It hides our cheeks and shades our eyes—

Was Blind but Now I See

Seventh grade means we're strutting our stuff and giving cheerleading our best. Mim-Mim and I have had routines since we were eight, and then Allie Rae came and added lots of pizzazz.

One afternoon after practice, I drop sweaty on the porch even though it's only March. I ask Sara to scoot inside and get me a Dr Pepper. When she comes back, she says, "Mama wants to see you right away."

I go in wondering what's what. Mama looks perplexed. "That was the school nurse on the phone. Calling about you."

"Yeah? What's up?"

Mama gives me a close inspection. "Myrtie says you squint. They've all noticed. Do you?"

Slouch, sure; squint, never. "Pitiful people squint, Mama. Not me. Why would Miss Myrtie say such a thing?"

"Myrtie is only trying to help, Sil, thinks we should have your eyes tested."

That's all I need. A vision test. "Mama, people who can't see aren't able to knock a bird out of the tree with a BB gun like—"

"I *told* you to cut that out," Mama shudders,

covering her ears. "I'm having your vision tested soon as possible. Myrtie says there's a good doctor over in Gilmer."

Thinking about that eye doctor frazzles me, but next week, I'm sitting in Dr. Kunesh's office reading the big-*E* chart. I am good on big *E,* but not much else. Dr. Kunesh talks all concerned, grandfatherly. "Are you sure that's all you can see, Silvy?"

"Yessir, but that *E* is clear as day. That means something, doesn't it?"

"It certainly does. I'm surprised you haven't gotten run over with vision as poor as yours."

Dr. Kunesh gets real buddy-buddy then, the way old people do when they're trying to butter you up. "Heh-heh, I think we can fix you right up, little lady. Let's call in your mama and pick you out a nice pair of glasses, shall we?"

Glasses??? Cheerleaders don't wear glasses!

Nervously, Mama comes in the examining room. "Is everything all right?" she asks Dr. Kunesh.

"Miz Lane, Silvy needs glasses. She needs them bad."

"This can't be. The whole family can see," Mama tries to convince him. (You tell him, Mama.) "Why she can knock a bird . . ."

"Needs them in a big way, Miz Lane. Without correction, people as nearsighted as your girl here are classified as legally blind."

Your girl? It sounds like I'm not in charge of me. Is this how the coloreds feel when they get called that?

"She must compensate beautifully," Dr. Kunesh
continues. All the while, he's unlocking a display case
of glasses. "I have to keep them locked," he explains.
"Poor whites and coloreds just walk in and help themselves to a pair. Pay what they can in eggs, butter,
when they can. Can't quite figure how they think
they can see outta these glasses. Don't have lenses."

I wonder what it feels like if no one ever really
sees you. Not being able to afford Dr. Kunesh's spit-
and-polish exams, the poor people pick out glasses
thinking any seeing's better than what they've got.

When I look in that display case, I near'about
faint. Row after row of ugly eyeglass frames stare
back. Dr. Kunesh seems partial to the gold-wire ones
my ancestors wore in their portraits. No wonder no
one cracked a smile. Then he has one or two kinda
neat-looking ones with rhinestones. "Well, if I have
to wear glasses, I'll take that red pair there with
rhinestones." Those might work for cheerleading.

Mama grabs Dr. Kunesh's arm and says frantically,
"She didn't mean that. Those glasses don't look any-
thing at all like what a twelve-year-old should wear.
Do you think?"

"Almost thirteen," I put in.

Dr. Kunesh nearly breaks his neck agreeing with
Mama. "Let's try these gold ones," he suggests,
polishing the old-lady rims on his white sleeve. He
balances the glasses on my nose and slides the wires
over my ears. "Now look at yourself," he instructs,
beaming.

I lean toward the mirror, but to tell the truth, I have to squint. Leaning closer, I look like an ad for vitamins. "No! No, I tell you, a thousand times *no!*"

"Maybe we'd better try something else," he now says directly to Mama. I, the customer, seem to have evaporated. He gives me a pair of tortoiseshells, and I shake my head. Next come some purple frames that make Mama groan. Finally, he tries a pair of pale blue plastic frames, very plain, no decoration.

While I examine myself in the mirror, Mama says, "We'll take those," without even asking her usual, "How much?" You'd think she had a Neiman Marcus charge.

Two weeks later, Mama and I drive back to Gilmer for the final fitting. Dr. Kunesh feels the frames around my ears and then puts the earpieces in hot sand. He shapes the frames until they don't pinch. "Wouldn't want to cause a ridge on your little nose," he says. "That should do it."

My little nose? All the while we are fixing my eyes, we are risking my nose?

When I'm finally fitted, Mama invites me to the Yamboree Drug Store to celebrate. As we walk there, the sidewalk seems to shift. Getting used to glasses will take some doing. After a double-chocolate banana split for me and a vanilla Coke for Mama, we start home.

The drive to Hughes Springs is amazing. I can tell horses from cows, read road signs. Just like the hymn said: "Was blind but now I see." I point to some live oaks. "Mama, I can see the new leaves coming on those trees. Not just green, but each *leaf* itself. Each one."

The next thing I know, Mama's pulled over on the side of the road. *Uh-oh,* I think, *flat tire.* When I turn to find out what's wrong, Mama's head is leaning on the steering wheel and she's sobbing. Her shoulders shake. "Mama, what's the matter? Did I say something wrong?"

Mama cries harder, really getting into it. When she finally reins herself in, she says, "Oh honey, why didn't you tell anyone you couldn't see? We could've done so much better by you."

When you can't see, you don't know it. You think that's how everything looks. "Mama, I thought everybody saw blurry."

"How could you not know?"

I look at the horizon, at the trees with their little chartreuse leaves, and wonder what else I missed. I've been going to a gunfight armed with a knife. "I just know I thought everything was okay; now I know it wasn't."

Mama puts the car in gear, and we head home.

I spend a lot of time looking. Now I can actually see twigs in the buzzards' nest atop the oak tree, not to mention the buzzards—bald, wobbly headed with Jello-y eyes—peering out at the world.

After most everybody has seen my glasses, all

comments favorable except Larry's "four-eyes" and Allie Rae's "wash-you-out," I begin enjoying my new vision. Most things look better, but downtown is older, dustier, than I'd thought. And the spigot where the coloreds drink is filthy.

"She Knows Her Place"

I keep thinking about what the Supreme Court
may do. Even the *New Era* has branched out from
obituaries to articles on how the Court can change
everything. If it happened, the law might let me and
Mabelee go places together. Even Allie Rae'd have to
come around if the law said so.

Saturday afternoon, I go behind Keasler's hoping
to show Mabelee my new glasses. She's nowheres in
sight, but there are more coloreds than I've ever seen
together before. Cookies, cakes, and pies are for sale.
It's almost a party. Uncle Hank's buying fried pies
like they're going out of style. Brother Posey sits at a
table with pencils and papers arranged in neat stacks.

Leafie, Miss Maggie's girl, and Eulalia, Tub's wife,
are sitting on nail kegs, passing the heat of the day.
Leafie and Eulalia share a piece of cake, jabbering
away. "Hey, Silvy, c'mere," Eulalia waves me over.

Eulalia has a baby on her lap. "That's about the
cutest baby I've ever seen," I say, and Eulalia answers,
"Sure 'nuff. Your new glasses lookin' nice, girl." Her
baby has eyes big as quarters and a crop of fuzzy hair
that shines halo-like where the sun hits it. Eulalia is
rocking him and humming some tune straight out of

a Tarzan movie. The baby gurgles, following every move his mama makes.

Eulalia takes a piece of cornbread and breaks off a chunk, chews it a bit, and swigs her soda. Then she sticks her finger into her mouth and removes a cornbread paste that she puts in the baby's mouth. The baby gums it, smiles, and drools. Finished, he opens his mouth like a little robin, hungry for more. It's about the sweetest thing I've ever seen.

But when I tell Mama, she is horrified. "I've told you and *told* you not to go hanging around the coloreds. And the nerve, selling their wares behind Papa's store!"

"I was just looking for Mabelee," I mumble. "She hasn't been around hardly since our how-to-do lessons."

Mama sighs. "That's because Mabelee has her *own* friends. *She knows her place.* Don't tell anyone what you saw, and stay away from places you don't belong. You hear?"

That's when I really begin watching what I tell Mama.

A Grass Widow among Us

These new glasses make me see things differently. At
home, Mama and Daddy hardly ever laugh together
anymore, and Daddy's lost in his own problems. I
don't even bring up wanting a horse.

When I ask for a ride to cheerleading practice,
I have to say, "Hey, Daddy," twice. He drives with
both hands on the steering wheel, eyes glued to
the road, and he answers my questions about work
with "Mmm." When I ask how his domino games
are going, he gives me a cold stare. "You're sounding
just like your mama," he says sharply. I'm glad when
we get to the football field.

Allie Rae and Mim-Mim are doing the Mustang
cheer—"Gimme an M. Gimme a U. Gimme an
S . . ."—when Allie Rae says, "Watch this." She
jumps up, grabs her knees, and pulls them over
her head, backwards, landing where she started.
"Hey, do that again," Mim-Mim says, eyes bulging.
"Suppose you could teach us?"

After cheering ourselves hoarse, we sprawl on
the grass, and Mim-Mim slips in a secret she overheard at the Fancy Curl. Seems like Miz Stookes told
Ella Mae that Bubba had gotten divorced!

Allie Rae adores it. "Run that by me again. Hey, Silvy, your grandmother's got more snap in her garters than you'd think, huh?" she snorts.

This is *huge* news, and coming from the Fancy Curl, it must be true. My grandmother *divorced*. I do not know one divorced person, unless it's Allie Rae's mother, Willie. And here trots up my own grandmother, a grass widow.

Isn't it just like my family to keep this a secret?

When I get home I intend to find out some things, but right away, I can feel a blue norther blowing our way. Something's definitely up between Mama and Daddy.

Mama's mind is off elsewheres; it's not a good time for talking. She gets me practicing the piano and sends Sara and Larry to do homework. It's hard to concentrate with her pacing.

After bedtime, over the wind, I hear the phone ring and put a glass to the wall to listen. Mama has a few mumbled words with somebody. Then she's on the phone again having a loud conversation with the domino hall. This late at night, Daddy should be here.

When Daddy gets himself home, Mama rushes out to meet him on the porch. "Jack!" she shouts, her voice so loud I'm afraid Miss Blue may hear. It sounds like he could use some help, so I jump out of bed and join them. "Hey, tone it down, would you?" Daddy says, pleading.

"Tone it down?" Mama's building steam. "You have some nerve."

Daddy looks like cold rain hit him. "What'd I do now?"

"Mama, Daddy just—" I say.

"You keep out of this, Silvy. Go back to bed." Then to Daddy: "Mother called twice today, and, imagine *this,* we're behind on our Keasler's bill *again.* It's so embarrassing. Ain't we pitiful? Poor us."

"Poor us, nothing. It's never us." My stomach gets shaky when Daddy's voice drops a notch. "The only time 'us' comes into it is between you and your mother. No wonder Mr. J. D. didn't call *me* about our bill. Course not, he'd take the family route, calling your mother who called you."

"Mama . . . ," I start, wanting to help Daddy.

Mama doesn't even notice. "I'm warning you, leave my family out of it." What's Mama mean? I thought *we* were her family.

Daddy continues as if she hadn't spoken. "I think I'm beginning to understand your poor father. Just another third wheel. One who hit the road."

Hit the road? He *left?* I sit on the steps, crying, not knowing how to stop them.

Mama rasps, "I mean it, Jack. Hush before you say something you shouldn't."

"So now you're telling me what I can say? Isn't *that* high toned? I've had enough." Daddy brushes past Mama and slams the door so hard I hear one of her figurines toddle off the piano and shatter. Mama follows him inside.

Daddy rushes back past me. This is terrifying, different from their usual fights. I call, "Daddy, wait," but in the wind, he must not hear. His truck peels out, gravel flying.

Mama joins me on the porch steps. She puts her arm around my shoulders, but I slough her off. I don't even want to see her. "Mama, you shouldn't of yelled at him like that." What if Daddy really meant it—that he'd had enough of us?

Mama breathes deeply. "Honey," she starts slowly, "sometimes parents argue. That's natural. It doesn't mean anything."

"It does to Daddy," I say. "Didn't you miss not having a daddy?" To be hateful, I add, "Or were you glad he left?"

Mama's eyes change from softness and regret to disgust. "Being a daughter doesn't give you the right to pry. Why not just pull my heart out?"

"What about mine? And Larry's and Sara's? What if he leaves us for good?"

"Oh, Silvy," Mama says, blankly. "He won't . . . and even so . . . you'd get used to it."

I go to bed and pull the covers over my head, but sleep is a long time coming.

Days go by with no word from Daddy. I call his work at the telephone company, planning to ask for a ride to cheerleading. Someone answers and says he'll call back. He doesn't. I wonder if he's safe. What if we never see him again? Unlike what Mama said, I don't get used to it.

Only Bubba goes on as usual.

The Lost South

Horses never spill the beans. Secrets go in their velvety ears . . . and stay. It's crummy not having a good-enough friend to tell things. Mabelee's someone I could've told about Daddy's being gone. We had lots of secrets once. We spit in each other's hand and promised not to tell forever.

Sleet hits the window. Those Yankees sent us a real norther this time. Weatherman says 1954 is the coldest late freeze since the chickens all froze back in the thirties. Spring usually gets going in late February, so April should do better than this.

Listening closely, over the ice bullets, I hear Mama and *Daddy*. Laughing! Daddy's back! My heart starts beating like a hummingbird's. When I run in the kitchen, they're having coffee like nothing ever happened.

Daddy is combing his tangled hair with his fingers. His eyes are bloodshot, and he could use a shave. Put Mama in a beauty contest with Miss Blue this morning, it'd be hard to judge the winner.

I hug Daddy hard. "I missed you." His eyes are blurry when he pulls me close, his sandpapery whiskers scratching my face. "I missed you too, Sis."

"Where were you, Daddy?"

You could've heard the pond evaporating.

Mama gives me a rumpled look. "You ask too many questions, Silvy. Let it slide." A book could be written on what our family leaves unsaid.

When Sara and Larry get up, people miles away can probably hear Sara shrieking "Daaaaddy."

At school, I want to celebrate Daddy's home-coming. But since no one knew he left, there's nothing to say. And then we fire up our main conversation, what's going on at the coloreds' school.

If we had nicknames that fit, Mim-Mim, who finds out everything, would be "Snoop." She leans close and confides, "Bet you didn't know Mabelee's teamed up with Jefferson, the big youth adviser, did you? They're going door-to-door our side of town selling baked goods, raising money for new books. Mr. Drugstore Williams shouted them off his place. Said 'git.'"

"Mabelee's selling over here!!?"

"Yep," Mim-Mim continues, "says it's for the Negro cause."

"Nee-gro?" Allie Rae mumbles. "Smart word." Even she's noticing that some words make some people squirm. Only *some* people. When I told Bubba that our Sunday school teacher said we should say "Negro" instead of "nigra," she said, "Fine! Nigra-o."

"What's wrong with the books we gave them?" I ask. "We used them, and they were all right for us."

Then I remember Mabelee's telling me about Paul Laurence Dunbar, the colored—make that Negro—poet. He surely wasn't in our books.

"Well," Mim-Mim says, "I listened in on Brother Posey's meeting back of Keasler's and learned that Jefferson has blueprints for a new school addition. Our old, used books would look right shabby there, huh? Mabelee and Alpha are smack-dab into everything."

I say, "Goldie will have a fit."

Mim-Mim chuckles. "You got that right. Miss Maggie's girl, Leafie, said Goldie isn't pleased a'tall. Course Alpha's always up for excitement, whether knife throwing or hunting, so he must be happy as a full tick. And then Mabelee, well . . ."

Allie Rae arranges her new poodle skirt. She's begun experimenting with clothes the way boys in Future Farmers of America experiment with electric fences. "Sounds like Jefferson can really stir up things with his little slaves. Happy times in the cotton patch, hoeing and singing, and singing and hoeing."

Mim-Mim looks like someone just farted at Miss Maggie's. "It's tacky to talk that way, Allie Rae. You know those slaves weren't happy. Many died making that cotton."

James Barnes and Duane join us. "This place has its own made-up history," James scoffs.

"Hold on a minute there, James," Duane says. "We come at things different here. And we were right sorry to lose Mr. Lincoln's war, even if slavery was wrong."

You'd think someone ran over James's foot with a tractor. "I can't believe you said that," he says. "Nobody here has respect for anything."

In Mr. Bollman's seventh-grade history class, we've been studying the Civil War. As we near the end of the school year, we near the end of the war. And that's when Mr. Bollman will give his "Lost South" performance.

Even though James isn't excited about Lost South, we wait expectantly. This big day nobody plays hooky 'cause Mr. Bollman's gonna act out the Civil War, marching and saluting, gasping and dying, the works. So on Monday, May 17, 1954, everyone's shoving, trying to get inside for a front seat.

The minute we're in the door, whoaboy. Mr. Bollman's red eyes and wrinkled suit make this Lost South different. Every year he paces before the blackboard, usually arriving dry eyed, with lots of gesturing and hand-wringing, till he gets to the South's surrender at Appomattox. Then he takes out his hanky and pretends to cry. This year it looks like he may *start out* crying.

You could hear a boll weevil yawn in this class-room. Mr. Bollman finally pulls himself together and begins, "I know y'all make fun of me and this lesson. I know that, but . . ." He wheezes like a dying man.

A few kids squirm. What's going on?

"But I'm here to tell you that the Lost South is not the past." He surveys the room. *"Not the past,"* he fairly shouts, "especially today." He chokes. Then he bows his head into a handkerchief and really, truly cries. His bony old shoulder blades hunch up like a sword on the battlefield. As his sobs get louder, his slick hair falls out of its Vitalis grip, and his fist pounds the desk, boom, boom, *boom*. "How could it ever happen?" he snuffles.

We watch for what seems like forever, and then James asks, "Mr. Bollman, sir, are you all right?"

"Am I all right?" Mr. Bollman clears his throat. "Am *I all right?* No, boy, I am here to tell you, I am not. No one will ever be all right again. News is now all over the airwaves. Today at one o'clock, the Supreme Court in its wisdom struck down 'separate but equal,' ruled in favor of the plaintiff Oliver Brown"—He spit out Mr. Brown's name—"and required the desegregation of schools across America."

The clock ticks loudly by the flag. George Washington watches from his portrait painted in clouds. We sit like statues, digesting this information. Duane lets out a low whistle. "This is big-time serious."

"You bet it is," agrees Mr. Bollman, nodding. "The South *is* the Lost South. Run along on home now, and remember how good you had it before some outsiders interfered."

Outsiders interfered. Jefferson's face flashes before

my eyes. I think about his coming here, making things happen. I picture Allie Rae and James with their different ideas. And I'm downright uneasy.

The school year ends shortly after Lost South. Brown vs. the Board of Education has everyone on edge. Even though the Court didn't say *when* our schools had to integrate, we all know a giant step's been made in a direction no one thought we'd go.

In town, Old Man Fulton stands on a crate shouting down Main Street, "We need us a few good lynchings." And then hopeful comments come from prayer circles that form by the dozens. Daddy says it'll take forever to mess with the South's schools.

Governor Allan Shivers agrees with Daddy. In Austin, he gets on the radio promising segregated schools for years because this ruling didn't provide a cure. But that doesn't answer the important question: What's going to be done about enforcing the law?

And when?

Some states plan to make their schools private. Charge money, say who can go. I think this is disgraceful and say so 'cause the coloreds don't have much money. Mama says in these times it's safer to keep my opinions to myself.

Daddy stands me, Larry, and Sara in a line. "Repeat after me," he instructs. "I will stick close to home."

"I will stick close to home," we promise, and I begin to believe we *may* be caught in a different kind of war.

"Cheery Dream"

Staying on Kingdom Hill gets so boring I start swatting flies. How enterprising can you be when you're stuck on a hilltop? I earn a nickel for every ten flies I get, and my admission to the picture show costs one hundred flies. I've got 'em piled in stacks of ten around the porch, waiting 'for the time Daddy thinks it's safe enough for us to leave home. Eventually even killing flies creatively gets boring.

So when Miss Maggie tells Bubba that my fingernails look like a redneck's, I arrange manicuring paraphernalia and call Allie Rae and Mim-Mim to come on up. They don't come from nervous homes like mine, so they can go anywheres. We begin filing, working our cuticles with orange sticks. Allie Rae reads my nail-polish label: "Hmmm, 'Cheery Dream.' A good omen, I should hope, better than keeping these fly corpses company. Flies laid out's so juvenile, Silvy."

Interrupting, Mim-Mim asks, "What you gonna wear the first day of eighth grade, provided of course the schools open?"

"Pull yourself together. For certain they'll open," Allie Rae says. "Just how much power you think the old Court has? I want to sit in the front row and wear plum eye shadow, but Willie says definitely not."

Mim-Mim squinches her face. "That's odd. Willie hardly ever says you can't do anything."

Allie Rae quickly defends her mama. "She *said* eighth grade's not for eye shadow. It's for making something of ourselves. That's why the school thing's important."

"Well, Willie sure makes something of herself, every time she hits Main Street," I say. "That dress she wore last Saturday goggle-eyed half the county."

"Wasn't it great?" Allie Rae says. "You realize we'll be the top of the heap for once in our lives?"

Mim-Mim almost cricks her neck agreeing.

While I'm dreaming of horses, currycombs, farriers, and saddle soap, they talk makeup, boys, and fashion. They smear Vicks salve on mirrors and practice kissing. When I try, it's like kissing a cough drop.

We have a cookout on my birthday. Nothing fancy, only us and Bubba. A few days ago, Daddy got a new job as a consignee with Gulf Oil Company. He delivers petroleum products and helps Gulf owners manage their gas stations. He drives up in his newly painted pickup—orange!—with the Gulf emblem and "Jack Lane 'That Good Gulf Gas'" on the doors. He has new Gulf clothes too. Crisp khaki pants and shirt, again with the emblem and his name on the pocket.

Daddy stacks logs in the oil-drum barbecue. It's a little hazy because the DDT truck sprayed this afternoon. Mama tries to party-up my party. "Just think Silvy, the *T* in *T-bone* stands for your thirteenth." She laughs and gives Daddy a hug.

Later, Daddy takes me for a special ride through town, just me and him, in his like-new truck. It's magical riding around with my handsome daddy, the wind whipping through my hair. Being with him, I feel everything will be okay.

Summer starts losing its grip. When I ride horses with Duane or cheer with Allie Rae and Mim-Mim, our shadows are longer.

The *Dallas Morning News* is full of stories about integration, letting Negro kids study with white kids. Some pictures in the paper show people marching and waving their fists. I think about Linda Brown going to a white school and wonder how it's working out for her.

Suppose the Court decided *our* town had to combine the schools? At the Lone Star café recently, Daddy heard talk about the Klan. Those hooded men haven't marched around here for years. And now there're whisperings about their coming back. "Why can't this be our chance to prove what we learn in church?" I ask Daddy.

"That's a good question, Sis. I don't really have an answer," Daddy says. "I doubt this world has one. But try asking your mama."

So I do. The question saddens Mama. "I used to wonder the same thing when I was your age, Sil. Things were happening then too, and it seemed like it might change. Then it got worse, and people got hurt, bad. So I began thinking, maybe this is better than that." Mama gives me a hug. "I'm sorry, honey, I wish we could live in a better, safer world. But we have to face the fact that although it isn't always pretty, it's not all bad."

That night I read from Mr. Dunbar's poem again.

> Why should the world be over-wise,
> In counting all our tears and sighs?
> Nay, let them only see us, while
> We wear the mask.

Big Scoops

The first day of school, Allie Rae phones and says, without even hello, "Meet me and Mim-Mim at Spring Park, okay? We'll walk together."

Allie Rae makes your eyes ache: bangling bracelets, a turquoise squaw-skirt with shiny braid that fans out like a lampshade. And Mim-Mim's wearing the plum eye shadow! She says she'll have her own makeup artist someday out in Hollywood. I'm not too spiffy decked out in a blue dotted-swiss dress from Keasler's.

Eighth grade turns out to be so boring I could get around with*out* new glasses! We've got only twenty-four kids in our class, most of them here since first grade.

Allie Rae starts griping when we're practicing cheering. She sprawls on the football-field bleachers. "I hear Jefferson's new school addition is going up at a steady clip," she says. "Even some white folks giving them money, thinking if the jigaboos *like* their school, they won't come to ours. Heard it's right nice, especially for them." Then she picks up her red and black pom-poms and starts the VICTORY cheer, alone. She jumps high in the air, kicks herself in the rear end, and punches the sky twice.

Mim-Mim's eyeballing a phantom crowd. Even she's begun ignoring Allie Rae's tacky talk. "You know," she says, "I've been thinking about selling those corny-dog coupons for football queen."

"Pass that by me one more time," Allie Rae says. "Why would we want to sell coupons when we're not even in high school running for anything?"

"It's how we do, Allie Rae," Mim-Mim explains. "We sponsor a candidate and sell coupons to help her win. *And* we get noticed for the money we raise. I say we help Tinky Stookes, a senior."

Allie Rae says, "Y'all do things funny, you ask me. How about instead of trotting around selling, we go in for one grand sweep. Think. Who controls the purse strings? And where's every female worth her salt on Saturday mornings?"

"The Fancy Curl," Mim-Mim says, brightening.

"Righto!" Allie Rae nods. "Like I say, we'll go there and let those corny dogs sell themselves."

Mama and Bubba say those big, puffed hairdos coming outta the Fancy Curl look like good hair gone bad. Even though they think it's a waste of time and money, Saturday morning finds me getting ready to go there. On our way to the beauty shop, Allie Rae says, "Well, look yonder." Mim-Mim gives a wave, and I call, "Hey, Mabelee, what's up?"

She answers dully, "Well hel-lo, Miss Silvy." Then she turns and walks away. Allie Rae mimics, "Miss Silvy."

Miss Silvy! Why say that? It's like she thinks I'm one of the ones trying to keep her in her place.

Allie Rae's still clucking when we get to the beauty shop. My insides feel like scrambled eggs. Was Mabelee being smarty, or did she think that greeting was funny?

At the Fancy Curl we're talking to Ella Mae, getting ready to put the sell on when the bell tinkles on the door. Miz Frances Stookes, Tinky's mama, comes in. She lives near the railroad tracks—the right side, she always points out—with her husband, LeRoy, and Tinky, their only daughter. We all like Tinky, but most everybody thinks Miz Stookes is so ugly-acting that her poor mama had to borrow a baby to take to church.

"And how are you?" Miz Stookes says to Miz Ellason, who's getting a wash and set.

"As well as can be expected this side of ten o'clock," says Miz Ellason without a flicker of emotion, "and with the news being what it is. I'm a good mind to stop reading the Dallas paper. We've always taken care of our coloreds. For the life of me, I can't see what they want."

I feel like shouting, "Cheerleading, they'd like cheerleading."

Miz Stookes nods. "It's that N-double A-C-P got everybody all swole up. Interfered in Virginia, South Carolina, now the Kansas thing decided in their favor. Don't get me wrong. I like a good nig same as anybody, but what*ever* was the Court thinking?"

"Yeah," Miz Stookes agrees, "they carried broad-minded way too far. You think anything'll happen here?"

"Looks like anything could happen anywheres," Miz Ellason sighs. "Guess we should just thank the good Lord it hasn't."

"You think we're safe?" Mim-Mim asks, her face askew, and I can tell she's mocking them.

"Don't you girls worry your pretty little heads about it," Miz Ellason reassures us. "Enjoy your school years. I was just blowing steam."

While Mim-Mim and Allie Rae start talking corny dogs, I'm still thinking about Mabelee. Would she even want to go to a white school like Linda Brown did? Would she have to call the white kids "Miss This" and "Mr. That"?

Miz Stookes begins flipping through a copy of *Bride's Magazine*.

"Why Frances, honey," Miz Ellason asks, "gonna have us a wedding?" She lights a Pall Mall, twirls that cig in her long, tapered fingers, and exhales with style.

Knowing a good thing when we hear it, we sit in the chairs by the beehive dryers to take it in.

Miz Stookes goes into overdrive. "Don't tell anyone, Hortense, but it looks like my Katrina'll be marrying a French diplomat."

"Do *what*? Where'd she find one?" Miz Ellason gasps.

"Right in our own backyard. He's a boy from Avinger, Travis Putnam."

A diplomat in our backyard? And Allie Rae thinks all the guys around here are common as pig tracks.

Miz Ellason gives Miz Stookes a sideways glance, sizing up the information. "Frances, honey, explain me this. Exactly how'd a French diplomat boy turn up in Avinger?"

Miz Stookes is not sidetracked one iota. "Well, he's fixing to be one, directly. Told Tinky when he gets himself out of diplomat school, they'll be living high on the hog in Paree, France," she continues. "A spring wedding would be nice, huh? Dogwood, azaleas."

"Do tell," Miz Ellason says through plumes of smoke.

"My grandbabies will be bilingual," Miz Stookes brags, "at ease with the world, if you know what I mean."

"At ease with all shades of foreigners is what you mean. Wouldn't any of those grandbabies be on their way anytime soon now, would they?" Miz Ellason asks.

We freeze in our seats. Tinky, pregnant?

Miz Stookes glares at the calendar. "I'm going to play like you never said that," she says, heading through the door and whamming it.

Miz Ellason splits a bobby pin with her teeth and looks our way. "Well, you girls hit the jackpot this morning, didn't you?"

You bet. Finally, I have a juicy tidbit to turn Mama's ears inside out. If only I can beat the telephone home.

I run as fast as I can.

When I get up the hill, Mama and Bubba are facing off at the kitchen table. Sitting stiffly, they are arguing about our school system.

"Guess *what?*" I say, catching my breath.

"Not now," Mama says, waving away my news. "I won't have it, these schools are awful." She points to me. "I asked her last week what she thought of Emily Dickinson's work, and you know what your granddaughter said?"

"No," Bubba says, leaning forward, getting ready.

"She *said,* 'Not much. I don't really like people from Daingerfield!' Can you be-lieve it? She thinks the poet Dickinson lives six miles down the road."

Bubba tries to help me. "Maybe they haven't studied Emily Dickinson yet."

"Maybe they haven't studied anything important."

"Oh, poof, you worry too much." Bubba dismisses Mama's view with a flutter of her hand.

I leap in with my mystifying news. "You will never ever guess what Miz Stookes told down at the Fancy Curl."

"In a minute, in a minute," Mama glosses over me.

"Mama, listen to me, will you? Miz Stookes told Miz Ellason that Tinky is getting married next spring to a French diplomat from Avinger." Surely I can drum up some interest; gossip is supposed to go better than this. "Miz Ellason got to wondering was Tinky perhaps p-g? What do you think about that? Huh?"

Mama shoots Bubba a petulant look. "See! That's exactly what I mean. No high-school senior has any business thinking about marriage. Our kids should be thinking about math and science and literature. Instead they're marching down the aisle prematurely, and . . . It's this crummy school system." She gasps. "Did you mean *pregnant?*"

"Probably not, cause Miz Stookes walked out. So I guess ol' Tinky and Travis are just *thinking* about doing *it*."

"Vulgarities," Bubba spits the word like a peach pit, "do not become women. Watch your mouth."

With the saddest eyes, Mama looks at Bubba. "There's got to be more. Here I worry all the time. Will the Gulf job last? Can Hughes Springs heat up any more if they force integration? I think maybe we'd be better off living somewhere with good schools, cultural opportunities. I've been reading about UCLA, the University of California at Los Angeles. It's a great school where our kids could make something of themselves."

"You're thinking of leaving?"

"Just thinking. I'm not sure this is the best environment to raise kids. And the schools, colored or white, are pitiful."

"They've always been good enough for *some* of us."

"But Mother, things are changing. California is a place of the future, not the past."

Bubba stomps her foot, a hissy fit brewing. "You

just want to get to California and look up your father. Well, Miss Highfalutin, it'd serve you right if you found him."

"How do you think that makes me feel?" Mama says, sounding stunned.

I am stunned. Did Bubba just let slip a family secret?

"Feel like you want. I'll talk however I please."

Bubba spins out of the room. She climbs into her car with great determination and leaves in a cloud of pink dust, tires screeching.

Honky Tonk Angels

Even though she's bossy, I miss Bubba's daily visits. But as usual on Sunday afternoons, she pulls into the side yard, honking wildly. Mama looks out but doesn't wave. Larry, Sara, and I run and pile in. Larry has his Davy Crockett rifle, and Sara whines, "He's shoving that thing in my side."

"Am not, am not, am not," Larry singsongs as Bubba drives. Riding around with them is just so embarrassing.

Bubba turns toward the back seat. "Pipe down back there or your children will be born naked." Ugh!

After going about a million miles and nearly landing in the ditch every curve, Bubba eases into a parking spot on the Dairy Queen's shady side. Draping her arm out the window, she signals a stop. At least she's quit saying "Whoa."

I glance at a Ford parked two cars down and see Allie Rae's long, soot-colored hair hanging out its window. She's propped against the car door, talking to the driver. Her head bobs in time to "Honky Tonk Angels" as the jukebox blares away. I can't believe it. My friend's talking to a boy, and I'm riding around with my squabbling family and a Davy Crockett rifle.

Larry and Sara fuss louder, and Allie Rae swivels her neck to the limit, giving us a bored stare. Her eyeballs look like marbles in a fishbowl.

"Hel-*lo* there, Allie Rae," Bubba chirps, waving. "You're looking well."

Allie Rae jerks to good-manners attention. "Uh, thank you, *thank* you. And how are *you?*"

"About the same," Bubba says, completely ignoring the boy with Allie Rae. "How's your mama these days?"

"Um, she's okay."

"Honky Tonk Angels" wraps up with a walk on the wild side while Bubba steps to the carry-out window and orders four medium Cokes. If I'm going to die soon, I hope it will be now on this spot. I keep sneaking peaks at Allie Rae and watching this handsome, dark-haired guy looking at her the way I know no one will ever look at me.

Allie Rae's friend seems pretty old, maybe sixteen or seventeen, in a pink and black shirt, hair slicked back in a ducktail, doing his level best to grow the broad, triangular sideburns I saw in *Life* magazine. A pair of blue and white fuzzy dice hangs from his rearview mirror.

Bubba opens the glove compartment and takes out softly melted Hershey bars. You'd think we are poorhouse bound the way we travel food around. She announces grandly, "Victuals fit for the gods."

When Bubba goes to get more paper napkins, Allie

Rae comes over. "You see that guy there? Name's Lonnie. From Daingerfield. Important thing is he can drive. And you know what that means?"

I know. She's been talking about nothing else for days. She has *got* to find herself a ride to the Louisiana Hayride, that place in Shreveport where singers do a stage show that the radio records.

"Well, I'm going, no two ways about it. You should too. This new guy Elvis is at the Hayride. Last week I listened, and he's really something. He moans while he sings. When you ask, don't tell all that, just say that Lonnie there drives good."

Bubba returns and begins passing out napkins. "Did you hear that commotion out back at the coloreds' window? Wouldn't you know it'd be Mabelee and some of her friends. Never heard such carrying on, celebrating the work on the nigra school, I suppose. I hear they've got a quote over the door: 'Education is the key to unlock the golden door of freedom.' George Washington Carver." Bubba takes a deep breath. "Half of those poor people won't be able to read that quote. And Mabelee's hair looked like her finger's in a socket."

"Mabelee's here? Why didn't she come see us?"

"Mabelee's tending to her own life, Silvy, the way you should tend to yours." Bubba starts the car and chirps to Allie Rae, "Toodle-loo, Allie Rae. Be sure to tell your mama I said 'hidy.'"

"Sure thing," Allie Rae says, grinning like a possum that's been found out.

We lurch out of the parking lot, the car making squealing noises, and Bubba says, "That boy's a Baptist, isn't he?"

"Just because the Ford dealership here belongs to a Baptist dudn't mean a thing. He's from outta town, Daingerfield."

My grandmother's idea of a mixed marriage is a Methodist who marries a Baptist. Although she'd never admit it, in her heart, I *know* she believes Jesus was Methodist.

"I happen to know, Miss Priss, that more separates Methodists and Baptists than trespasses and debts."

She's going on like this because Daddy was a dipped Baptist before he married Mama. Even though he's found out that he's getting his own Gulf station—how much better can he do?—Bubba still has nothing good to say about him. "Bubba, don't you like Daddy? At all?"

She turns and looks right through me, like a cat. "I'll say this for him, he's as handsome as they come, and charming. But my heavens, he loves a party. Only man I ever knew who actually enjoyed World War II."

I feel my dander getting high as Mama's. "For your information, that mail ship he was on sailed through an ocean full of mines. He could have been blown sky high, eaten by sharks."

Bubba grimaces; a bird could sit on her lip. "He brought home a right smart amount of money, and it wouldn't surprise me if he played cards on a sunny deck to get it. But to answer your question, yes, I like your daddy, in spite of a lot. And I'm proud that his enterprising's finally starting to work. 'Bout time. Now, what were you and Allie Rae discussing so earnestly back there?"

Larry chimes in, "They wanna go to the Louisiana Hayride next Saturday night and see Mr. Elvis. He moans when he sings."

"Say *what?*" Bubba says bristly. "My stars, turn your back to enjoy a Co-Cola, you never can tell what'll happen."

"Nothing happened," I pout. "Shut up, buster."

"We never say 'shut up' to our loved ones," Bubba says. I scoonch down in the car seat and adjust the sidewing window to blow air into my face. She pokes my shoulder. "Don't slouch. Anybody can get married but a hunchback."

Oh, me, no words can continue this fiasco. Bubba drives up Kingdom Hill, and I can't get out of the car fast enough. Mama's peeking out the dining-room window.

An iron-ore sunset begins forming. Bubba heads for home as bats begin ushering in evening. Inside, Mama's waiting for a full report.

"Mama," I say, trying to figure out a way to ask, "if we have a good, safe driver, do you suppose I could go see a stage show that's being put on the radio? I think it'll be real educational."

Mama eyes me cautiously, but also smiling a little. "What's this really about, Silvy?"

"Allie Rae and probably Mim-Mim and about everyone else's going to the Louisiana Hayride next Saturday night, and you know, it really would be something to see a live radio show."

"Silvy, I may look too old to know anything at all, but I have heard of Elvis. Excitement follows him around. All that shaking and moaning and what he calls music is beyond me. I'm sure your daddy and I could find a decent radio show to take you to sometime."

But I don't want a proper show! To console myself, I say, "Aw, Elvis is probably a hick who won't amount to a thing."

Often in error, never in doubt.

Mama gives me a squeeze. "Having a daughter is great. You make me feel thirteen years old myself. Your grandmother and I spend a lot of time trying to teach you manners because we want to make you our legacy, a true lady who'll follow us."

So that's it, a true-lady legacy. Following them. Like them? I used to think I'd rather kiss a pig. Now, I'm not sure. "Mama, why don't y'all work on Sara?"

"Oh, we do, Silvy, we do. Some people just take more work, no offense."

Easy Street

Mama's planning Opening Day for Daddy's Gulf station. There'll be orchids for the ladies, cigars for the men, and orange suckers with Gulf logos for the kids.

Daddy spends hours on the phone with the Gulf big shots who'll come from Houston. With business going well, he's planning three more stations in other counties. He and Mama are saying "us" a lot these days, like they mean it. Our new address may be Easy Street.

Opening Day ceremonies are scheduled for ten o'clock on a Saturday in late October. Limbered up and running smooth, Mama gives me a hug. "Wear your new dress and make your daddy proud, okay?"

Okay!

Downtown, a huge banner stretches across Main Street: "That Good Gulf Gas." Balloons bob everywhere. In the distance, the band's playing. As Allie Rae, Mim-Mim, and I make our way through the crowd, Allie Rae's still pushing the Hayride. "Trust me, this Elvis's terrific," she explains, gyrating. "The Pelvis."

I spot Mama with her hair fluffed almost Fancy-Curl-like, and Daddy's puffing a cigar like a millionaire.

His grin reaches all the way to his eyes. He whispers something to Mama, and she puts her head on his shoulder.

The mayor taps the loud speaker and begins a long speech about our distinguished visitors from Houston, blah, blah, blah, blah. When he winds down, Mr. Jacobs, one of the big shots, says some kind things about Daddy—what big plans Gulf Oil has for him.

I make my way over to Bubba, who's standing nearby. "Hey, Bubba, wasn't it great, what they said about Daddy?"

She stammers, "Yes. Yes, it was. Tell your mama she did a nice job getting these festivities in order. And your daddy too, of course."

"Bubba, you tell him. And Mama. She's not mad at you. She's just Mama."

The big shots start giving away cigars.

Daddy and Mama pass out the orchids, and when Daddy said orchids for all the ladies, he meant *all* of them. The Negro ladies wear the flowers like jewelry, admiring themselves in the plate-glass windows. I'm having a Dr Pepper when I see Mabelee.

She's walking with Jefferson, hanging onto his every word. Postmaster said, when his new books arrived, they were all about Negro people—Sojourner Truth, George Washington Carver, Langston Hughes—and they told all the good stuff Negroes do.

Mabelee looks like a tropical princess with two

orchids, one on each shoulder of her shiny red dress. "Wow, girl, look at you," I say. "Ain't you looking fine, Mabelee?"

"Ain't I ever?" Mabelee agrees, giving a little curtsy with a hint of fun back in her eyes.

She raises her hand, and I think we are going to touch, but we don't. Then Mabelee laughs her old laugh, clear as a running creek. "This here's Jefferson, 'member me telling about him? Helping with the MYF, then the school? Now, he's teaching it. We're learning good things."

Jefferson smiles with charming eyes and extends his hand. "Pleased to finally meet you." Up close, he's what everyone says, starched and straight and proud. What hereabouts is called "uppity," but he's mighty fine.

Buckrod's watching, polishing his star with his thumb. "Hello, Jefferson," I say, not shaking his hand or nothing with Buckrod there. Jefferson seems to understand and nods. I've touched Goldie and Mabelee all my life, but now . . .

Mabelee waves and flounces down Main Street. She swishes her skirt with style. A *lot* of style.

Allie Rae says, "That little nig is one sassy twitchy-britches. Hear her friend's a troublemaker too. Stirring things up."

Mim-Mim frowns, her voice scunnered. "Oh, Allie Rae."

Inside, I get a watch-it feeling. I've tried to overlook

Allie Rae's uglified talk, but this's a fine howdy-do on my daddy's big day. "Allie Rae, Mabelee's been my friend a long, long time. In the future, keep her name out of your mouth. Got it?"

From Allie Rae's expression, you'd think I slapped her. "Oh, ho, guess I've been told. How about you, Mim-Mim? You in the same pew?"

Mim-Mim puts her finger to her temple, thinking visibly.

C'mon, Mim-Mim! Six perfect-attendance years in Sunday school should teach you something.

Finally, she stares at Allie Rae point-blank. "Guess I am, Allie Rae, most certainly guess I am."

Allie Rae throws her orchid in the street and stomps it. "I'll head on over to the funeral home then, where people like me. Some people *do* like me, you know."

Watching her disappear down Main Street, I see a lot of good times going with her.

Mim-Mim seems to be struggling with this falling-out too. "Don't feel too bad. We didn't invite her not to come back. She'll get over it, you know how fighty-fied she is."

After our great Opening Day, Mama invites Bubba to supper. She's sending a strong message—we're not moving anywheres. Eagerly, Bubba accepts.

Leftover suckers and orchids are at everybody's place, good feelings so strong you can nearly touch them. Mama and Daddy keep reliving the day. This gets Bubba going on one of her old stories. "You know when Papa started the store, he got pretty good at judging character. Papa always said, 'Never trust a man who prays in public.' Exactly what that Jacobs man did today."

The smile freezes on Mama's face. "Don't ruin this night for us, please."

"Wouldn't dream of it," Bubba says. "But think about it. Nobody asked Mr. Jacobs what plans they had for you. He just ups and prayed in public."

The moment passes, but Mama doesn't look as happy as before.

"Lots of Kinks Need
to Get Ironed Out"

"I've been thinking, Jack," Mama says, "you know when Mother and I got in our tiff the other week? She is the fatiguing-est woman. It started with our deplorable schools, and blossomed."

"That so?" Daddy asks, not much paying attention. "It'll work itself out . . ."

Mama charges ahead, worrying *how* it will work itself out. "Can you believe that our children are subjected to teachers like Sim Addison? That man couldn't teach a hen to cluck. He told Larry's class that gravity caused night and day!"

"Don't get yourself wrought up," Daddy says, eyeing his newspaper.

"Wrought *up*?" Mama asks, aiming for reasonable-sounding, but missing. "Our children will have to compete with the educated people of this world, people who know why the sun rises and sets. They need more, if they're going to get college educations. And don't tell me I'll be wanting the moon next."

"Wouldn't dream of it." Daddy puts the paper away.

Mama zooms to her point. "I've decided you should run for the school board. Slot's been open since Mr. Jud died. And our schools need good people at the helm more than ever."

Daddy rises halfway out of his chair. "Why on earth would I get myself into that?" he groans.

"Now don't get *your*self wrought up," Mama teases, getting in the last word. "I'll start work on your campaign."

Daddy holds his head in his hands, his lips moving silently.

Running against nobody, Daddy wins by a landslide. On the third Monday night of each month, four board members and the school superintendent meet to discuss school business.

After Brown vs. the Board of Education, the meetings are swamped with people against integration. Things are fine the way they are, they say.

"What did you do?" I ask Daddy, after his first meeting.

Daddy explains like a statesman. "I just said, 'No call to get riled up, everybody. Nothing's happening here any time soon. Lots of kinks need to get ironed out of that ruling.'"

And that was that, he says. Next Daddy brought up Mr. Addison's teaching technique, and the board moved to interview Mr. Addison next month.

Thanksgiving nears and Allie Rae still doesn't look our way. Nothing's much fun without her, so when Mim-Mim calls and says, "Let's meet at the Lone Star café," I quit moping and join her.

Mim-Mim sits at a booth, flipping through

jukebox selections. "Hey," Arnold calls from the counter. He's wearing a dingy hat right-angled to his eyebrows and a grease-spattered apron.

"I felt like a chicken-fried steak sandwich," Mim-Mim says, "already ordered. How about you?"

"Just a strawberry malt and fries," I call to Arnold who begins talking to the grill as he starts our orders.

A new, crisp sign hangs over the counter: "We Reserve the Right to Refuse Service to Anyone." We never had signs like that before. Negroes around here knew what they were supposed to do, and so did we.

"I bet I grow old and die sitting right here waiting for something to happen," Mim-Mim begins, choosing "Good Rockin' Tonight," a new Elvis hit on the jukebox.

"Quit whining, Mim-Mim." It's hard to pay attention to her with that sign in plain sight. How would Mabelee feel if she saw it? She'd probably mouth off, and Arnold would broomstick her outta here, paying customer or not.

"I can see it now," Mim-Mim says, moony-eyed. "I'll be an old lady in pink curlers, rushing through Piggly Wiggly to get supper on the table. Three or four snotnosers hanging on my skirt tail."

"Forget it. You're Hollywood bound."

"Oh *yeah,* I'll sit under palm trees, wear strapless Hawaiian dresses, and everyone will have manicured toes, even the men. Those manicured men fall at my feet. . . ."

Arnold puts our orders before us. "Here you go, ladies," he says, almost flirty. That gets us giggling. Mim-Mim frowns when he returns to the grill. "See that phone over there?" she says. "We could call up Allie Rae. And . . . ," she pauses.

She's the longest pauser.

"And what?"

"And maybe we'd find out she misses us too." Mim-Mim clicks her fingernails on the table. "We have nothing to lose. Let's do it."

Mim-Mim dials the funeral home. Her face lights up. "Hey, Allie Rae," she says, so happy. "Silvy and I were just thinking about you, wondering if we might come over Saturday night and listen to the Hayride together? Uuum, Allie Rae? Allie?"

"What happened?"

"Said for us to listen to the Hayride our ownselves. And have fun. She hung up on me!"

Feeling low, we leave the Lone Star and head down Main Street. Mim-Mim goes home and I aim for Keasler's.

Mabelee's standing near the alley. She waves me over. "Miss Silvy, can I speak to you a sec?"

"Hey, Mabelee, how's it going?" Is she serious, Miss Silvy again? When I get nearer, I see why. Jefferson steps out of the alley, dressed like a businessman. He moves into our conversation. "Miss Silvy, may I have a word with you?" He tips an imaginary hat. "Since your father's now on the school board, I was wondering if he might be open to a proposal from us."

Red lights go off in my head: DANGER, DANGER, stop.

Mabelee, a little shamefaced, begins falling all over herself explaining. "Silvy, it's a small thing really, not us coming to y'all's school or nothing. You know that new football stadium you got? We'd like to clean up your old one—no one's using it ever—even pay some rent. Then we could have football games our ownselves on a real field. I could be a cheerleader. Jefferson says maybe you'd kinda suggest it to Mr. Jack. If he could get us into a meeting, we could do our own asking."

Jefferson's so polite and Mabelee's so eager, I want to say sure, but Mabelee's troubles aren't my fault. I didn't cause them. Daddy'd be furious at me for getting involved, and the whole town would be suspicious. They might think Daddy was pushing integration.

"Well, Miss Mabelee, Mr. Jefferson," I say slack jawed.

Mabelee looks shocked. I'm feeling polite and proper myself, and I hear some of Mama's and Bubba's words fly out of my mouth. "You've caught me by surprise. It's an interesting idea I'll think about."

Their faces fall. They know. "Got to go," I say and run out of there like greased lightening. I hear Mabelee calling behind me, "Silveeee, please, I want to be a cheerleader, same as you."

"Our Kids Could Do Worse"

Coward. Pure and simple. I don't mention the request
to Daddy. Sure, I think Mabelee deserves to be a
cheerleader. She's louder than a banshee. And I think
it'd be fair if she went to school with us someday.
But do I lift a finger to help her? No. The next school
board meeting comes up and Mr. Addison's stupid
teaching technique is on the agenda.

Daddy tells Mama about the meeting on the night
the radio says we'll have our first frost. I'm bundled
up on my eavesdropping porch step wondering if
Mabelee and Jefferson might've gone to the meeting
without my help.

"At first, the meeting made me nervous, complaints flying everywhere about the coloreds' new
youth adviser. Mabelee's new friend can sure stir
up things." Definitely no Mabelee or Jefferson at
this meeting! "Some complaints about their new
books full of colored heroes. I think some folks
are worried they'll fix up better than us. Even
with the unrest, I believe our schools are in pretty
good shape," Daddy says softly. "And, you know,
Sim Addison's not such a bad sort at all. I liked
him."

Sharp as a scorpion's sting, Mama's reply rings out, "Liking's not the point."

Daddy doesn't back off. "He was pitiful when he came in. Wore his Sunday suit and carried his hat out in front of him, fixing to bolt. Talked about gravity and has night and day down pat. He says he just likes to use fascinating subjects creatively."

"He's one of those people, every time you try to hang, the rope breaks," Mama says.

Daddy says, "You know what I think?"

After a few swing creaks, Mama asks, "What?"

"I think our kids could do worse than Sim Addison. A lot worse."

"You may be right, but it's so frustrating for me. Let's go inside, I'm cold."

Watching the hoarfrost settle this November evening, I make a wish: Let someone solve the school problems as well as Daddy solved Mr. Addison's. Let Mabelee get bunches more new books. Let things get better.

The next day, I head to Bubba's hoping for a Coke. Instead, I find Goldie standing at a dishpan of soapy water, singing like a funeral soloist. "Hey, Goldie," I call.

"Silvy," she says, with no greeting at all. She drones on, "Just a closer walk with Thee . . ."

"You okay, Goldie?"

"I'm here, ain't I?"

"You seem down."

"I got plenty reason to be draggin'. Mabelee's like somebody I don't know no more. Got Alpha in the middle of ever'thing. Running around with Jefferson getting into who-knows-what kinda messes."

"I met Jefferson in town the other day. He seemed okay."

"Don't get fooled, Silvy. That college boy spells trouble, waving his book learning around. He excites people, and really he don't know 'what' from 'how many.'"

"I thought they were getting things done at your school."

"Huh!" Goldie says, "Me, I count on the good Lord to get things done. Not Jefferson."

"I'm sure Mabelee'll be fine," I say, but I'm not.

When I leave, she starts another song. I hear it a long ways, and it piles more dreariness on this day.

What's next?

Remember As You Pass Me By

At first, I can't tell what's happening.

Mabelee and I are in the chicken yard under the privet hedge, not far from where we suspect Bom's insides are buried. Mabelee's sweeping the playhouse, complaining about Alpha and her little brother, Omega. "Boys never do no work," she's saying when the grave cracks open and Bom's insides start spilling out. Mabelee screams, "Silvy, *Silveey,* help! They're gonna get me!"

I sit up in bed. What time is it? Is sleet scritching the window? "You there? Open the window, please, Silvy. I need help, bad."

Seeing Mabelee's face pressed against the screen, I raise the window. Cold air rushes in. "That you, girl?"

"Course it's me. Who else come tearing up this hill, needing a safe place to stay? It's freezing out here."

A *safe* place to stay? "You shouldn't of come here."

"Silvy, you won't believe what's going on. Buncha men come riding through looking for Jefferson and Alpha, screaming ugly, scary things. Going door-to-door. We were working late at the school, got outta there just in time. I surely don't know what to do. You the onliest one I know can help me."

Worry creeps over me. She's serious. "But it's *not* safe here. Even my daddy's worried about what's going on. He hears you and—"

"That's exactly why it *is* safe. Nobody'll think we'd come to Whitetown!"

"We?!!!" The farther she gets into her story, the worse it begins sounding. Who else is with her? Jefferson? Daddy'll jerk a knot upside my head if he finds me speaking to that smooth-talking man. He's already said as much.

"Just me here, now," Mabelee answers, her voice steadying. "Jefferson and Alpha waiting, uh—"

"Keep it down, would you? Go wait in the lot. I'll be there in a jif." I pull on jeans, a sweater, double socks, and jacket and ease out on the porch. Voices drift up the hill, maybe across town, from the Bottom. Loud mean voices, angry. Looking over the treetops, I see dots of fire moving in a line! What has Mabelee gotten herself into?

Out back, Mabelee hunches against the wild cherry tree. Her teeth are chattering. "You wouldn't believe it, you surely wouldn't, Silvy. Seen it with my own two eyes . . ."

I pat her back. "What happened?"

"Everything was going so good. They let us get the school addition finished—painted, new books— before they hit us with their evil. How long you suppose they been planning this? Since the Supreme Court ruled for us?" She takes a deep breath.

"And Jefferson he kept teaching about our people who made a difference, said we could make a difference too. Yes! Like Jesse Owens says, 'One chance is all you need.' *One* chance is too good to hope for, I reckon. Even Alpha started reading books."

"Where's Alpha now?" I'm a little afraid of the answer, and when I hear it, my teeth start chattering too. "What'd you say?" I croak.

"In the graveyard, Silvy. Both 'em. We were running to get you, cutting through the graveyard when Alpha, he stepped on a nail. He needs bandages bad, Silvy. Jefferson stayed with him, didn't think coming up here was a good idea nohow. Last I saw, they was hiding next to that scary grave marker, you know the one."

"Surely they could of made it outta the graveyard. He hurt that bad?"

"'Spect so. Nail went clean through his shoe into his foot, bleeding right smart when Jefferson pulled it out. Pretty good hiding place, you ask me. Nobody goes to a graveyard at night, in winter to boot. 'Spect Mr. Fulton with those men looking for us. Think I heard his voice."

"Oh, Lordy. Did you see anybody else?" This can't be happening. I know everybody in town and picture neighbors, friends, most sweetly in their pews. Faraway voices scrub through the night.

"Um, well, nobody much," she hesitates. "Maybe your uncle, Mr. J. D. White folks at night all look the same. White. Probably Mr. Drugstore Williams, and somebody sounded like it could be Buckrod."

"That's awful. He's supposed to keep the law."

Mabelee starts crying. "There's no law out there tonight. Not for us anyways. They got torches and clubs. Some guns. Hollering hateful things. It's one sorry sight. And all we wanted was a good school. Like y'all. Learn about us. Like y'all do y'all."

"Hold on, Mabelee. I'm going back in the house for bandages, and then we gotta think of something quick."

Sneaking inside creaks every floorboard. After a record-breaking noisy tiptoe, I find iodine and clean rags for bandages. Where could they hide? An old fishing camp? A duck blind? The City Dump? When I get back to Mabelee, she looks like a night watchman. "You hear that?" she asks. "Phone maybe?"

A light comes on in the house, making dim patches of yellow in the yard. That *was* the phone. "We gotta move, fast," I say, pulling her along.

Running down the hill, we hear Daddy's pickup heading toward town. Mabelee pushes me into a plum thicket. That phone call must've been for Daddy, but where is he going so fast? This late?

At Miss Blue's, I think I see her curtain move. If she sees me helping Mabelee, I'll be in an awful jam. We cut through backyards and down side streets. At Bubba's, all is quiet. Four blocks farther, we cross the highway and sneak onto the cemetery road.

The crushed-shell driveway crunches loudly till we get inside the wrought-iron gates protecting the dead. Night voices have leveled off. We make it to the scary tombstone and catch our breaths.

Remember as you pass me by
As you are now, so once was I
As I am now, you soon shall be
Prepare for death and follow me.

"They been here. See?" Mabelee says, running her hand over the marker. "Blood, and a good bit too. They must be 'round somewheres. Jefferson, you there? Alpha?"

I see them first. Coming out of the Keasler lot!

Mabelee runs to them, snuffling, and Jefferson tells her to hush up. "This may not be one of your better ideas, Mabelee," he says sternly.

Jefferson is beginning to look like the Negroes around here. His clothes are wrinkled, his posture slumped. He scowls, "I thought we could change things, but after tonight, I don't think help from whites is—"

Mabelee cuts him off. "She's trying to get us outta this fix!"

I look at the graves. "You should be safe here for a while. You've got good company. Let's not disturb poor Bom and Papa's peace."

"*Who?*" Jefferson blinks.

"These here dead white ones." Alpha fills him in, pointing. "I spent many hours sweating on this lot. Working it to be pretty."

Alpha has some gall. I remember summers when he was so lazy he followed shade around the house. "It's not like you volunteered to do it, Alpha, it was your *job*. A job lots of boys would've appreciated."

Jefferson's eyes bore into me, all business now. "See Mabelee? We should be grateful. They're all alike."

Alpha bends over his bandaged foot, moaning. "Sorry, Silvy. You been good to us as you know how."

"As she knows how, huh! She'll probably help us tonight like she helped us with the school board," Jefferson scoffs. "They're doing the best they can, they don't know better."

Before I can answer what Jefferson is saying about me, about all of us, an explosion rocks the night. My eardrums vibrate. We turn toward the Bottom and see the sky fairly dancing with orange. It looks like a watercolor painting done on too-wet paper.

"Oh, no," Jefferson moans, "that's the school." He begins pacing, his head low. I feel his anger like the fire we're watching. Then anger turns to sorrow. Not too many males cry; he's only the second one I've seen, after Mr. Bollman.

"We'll be okay, Jefferson," Mabelee whispers, holding his shoulder, crying her own tears. "I *told* you we were taking a gamble, trying new things. Silvy is our chance to get outta here."

"You have any plans?" I ask, and am surprised to hear Jefferson reply without any tears in his voice.

"If we can make it west to Daingerfield and up to Rocky Branch, we'll be okay. There's a church brother who'll hide us, then get us on to safety. It's getting to Rocky Branch that's the hitch. A good fifteen miles on Alpha's bummed foot."

"I've got it!" I say. "The night train goes west in a couple of hours. It'll cross over at Veal Switch and stop at Rocky Branch."

Jefferson opens his mouth and nods his head. He says slowly, "It might work. Yes, Lord, it just might. But where'll we hide till we hop that train?"

I say, "It stops behind Keasler's, so . . ."

Mabelee whines, "Oh, no, you don't, Silvy. You ain't getting me in there. No way. I've known that place's haunted for years. They used to lock us in there before they lynched us in the woods. Now spiders and bugs mix with those ghosts."

"Where's that?" Jefferson asks. "Hush, Mabelee."

"The calaboose," I whisper. "Never in a zillion years would anyone look there. Not used forever. Train stops between the calaboose and Keasler's."

"Never thought I'd see the day I'd be listening to some white girl convincing me to go to a calaboose. Jailed," Jefferson says, watching the sky now billowing with sparks.

Alpha stands on his good leg like a stork, puts his face into Jefferson's, and says, "Might sound strange, brother, but you know what, it might be *our* one chance."

"Oh, me," Mabelee says with fear-tinged resignation. She begins praying, wringing her hands.

I shake Mabelee. "Right now we have to move! And we gotta help Alpha. His foot's a mess."

Alpha hobbles between Jefferson and Mabelee, slinging an arm over each. Mabelee prays with every step. Finally, we start down the railroad tracks.

Funny what you remember. Mabelee's best roles play like a picture show. I see us sneaking off here, putting crossed nails on the tracks, hoping the train will mash them into tiny scissors. Her in rain, singing, "Jesus is peeing, he's tenderly peeing, peeing for *youuuu* and for me," her head thrown back, the water balling up on her braids. Mabelee lifting a tea-party cup, little finger hiked, wondering if tea were really tee? Holding herself down below because she giggled so hard.

Tonight's no game. I trade places with Mabelee, and me and Jefferson become Alpha's crutches. We slowly reach the alley behind Keasler's and make it back to the calaboose. A shiny chain hangs around the door.

The calaboose is locked!

"Now what?" asks Jefferson, disgusted.

In the distance, the train chuffs and blows. Jefferson looks relieved. "Our train must be early so we won't need to hide."

"Think again. That's the eastbound train, Jefferson. Take Alpha's knife and start working on that lock."

Mabelee stops praying and faces me. "Silvy, would you do me one more thing?"

"What?" My voice sounds shrill in this night that may never end. The train whistle blows louder.

"Go tell Mama me an' Alpha will be okay. Tell her she'll be hearing. Do that for me, Silvy. All right? She's probably worrying herself sick."

She's right. But Goldie won't be the only one worried sick. I can be in a mess if Miss Blue saw me and puts out the word I'm helping Negroes tonight.

Though it's dangerous, I owe Goldie. Who always took care of us, and held me on her bony lap? And I owe Mabelee. Who danced around the chinaberry tree, while Goldie wrung a rooster's neck, singing "Rooster, we do what we must"?

"Okay," I agree, as the eastbound train slows beside us, "but I've gotta leave now. This train will take me to Turkey Creek. I can make it to your house from there and get myself home by morning."

"Be careful," Jefferson says sheepishly, "and thanks."

"Yeah," I say, wondering if I'll ever see Mabelee again. She touches my arm lightly, I feel her shaking, and she leaves. I watch her disappear as long as I can.

Night-Train Lessons

Riding that train makes my heart pound harder than riding trees. Pulling up into a boxcar, I lay low as it passes through the Bottom with the colored school burning. Sure enough, Old Man Fulton is the hit of the evening. Everyone's his buddy tonight. I see their outlines against the fire's light.

When the train slows at Turkey Creek, my head is reeling. I definitely saw Buckrod and Mr. Drugstore Williams and am glad I didn't see Uncle J. D. Mabelee's seeing him doesn't surprise me though. It makes me cringe.

And where *is* Daddy?

When I roll off the train, I find the lane going to Goldie's and start through rows of rickety, leaning shacks. Trash blows everywhere, and the outhouses smell like polecats. Out here are no cars, no telephone or electricity wires.

I haven't ever been to Goldie's, but Bubba has. Long ago, I woke up to find Mabelee sitting on my bed, crying. She said their baby, Omega, had colic so bad that Goldie thought he'd die—he sounded like a bullfrog in clabber. Holding her nose, Mabelee'd "KA-WONK"ed loud enough to scare a bullfrog.

My grandmother'd gone into action, collecting materials for mustard plasters and all the medicine she could find. She'd driven Goldie and Mabelee home in the middle of the morning, not just down the hard road, all the way there.

All the way here. I can't imagine Bubba coming down this lane with supplies that Goldie claimed saved Omega's life. What did she say? "I am so sorry. I didn't know this."

But she did. Bubba knew!

In some of these houses, kerosene lamplight shines through cracks. You could freeze with these walls.

Bubba'd said Goldie's house is at the end of the lane. Trees tunnel overhead and night creatures chorus. Up a ways, there's another fire. Did the mob come here looking for Jefferson and Alpha? Goldie's yard is full of people, and someone's singing low.

Dogs set up a squall. I've never heard such baying, and I'm afraid. Eerily, the singing stops. "Who's there? That you, Mabelee? Alpha?" Finally, a creaky voice chimes in, probably Goldie's mama, Old Miss Violet, "Them dogs don't bark at our babies," and a deep voice booms, "Where's my gun? Git it, Cyrus."

"Don't shoot," I yell, hoarsely, "it's Silvy. You know me. Silvy from Whitetown."

"I'll swan," Goldie says, "what you doin' here, chile?"

In the firelight I see nervous-looking people. "I came to tell you Mabelee and Alpha left town for a bit. Said you'd be hearing." Old Miss Violet sets up a wail, and Goldie exclaims, "I *knew* it."

"With Jefferson," I explain, "on the night train. They had to go."

"Got no business on no train," Goldie says. "Got no business changing everything neither. I said all along that boy'd lead my babies to no good. And now look. Who brought you out here, girl, this time of night?"

"I took the train myself." I feel proud until Old Miss Violet picks up steam, increasing in volume. "There's trouble in town," I continue, and they nod their heads.

"We know," Goldie says. "We heard."

Apparently, news travels fast between Goldie and her neighbors too. "Good evening, Miss Violet, Goldie. You take care, you hear. I'd best be getting on."

"That's downright frightful," Goldie says. "It's not safe for no white girl out here tonight. Ain't safe for nobody nowheres tonight." She waves over a huge black man who must weigh about a ton. "Axel here's my neighbor, trust him with my life. With my girl too," she adds gently, rubbing my cheek with the back of her hand. "Axel been knowing ever' creek bed and holler for miles. He git you home safe, the back way, on his mule."

Axel has a kind face and when he lifts me astride, I feel dainty as I've always wanted to be. "Okay?" he asks. You'd think he's inquiring about seat cushions instead of some mule's bony behind.

When I ask if he's riding too, Goldie shakes her head. "That would never do, Silvy. Think. Black man, white girl together on a mule. No siree, Axel he's pulling."

We take off into the woods at a steady clip. Axel stops in gullies, listening, and his head swivels like a hoot owl's. At the edge of town, he leaves me off beside the water tower, just below Kingdom Hill. When I thank him, he tips his cap and fades into the dark.

Without a flashlight I feel my way up the hill. It's eerily quiet, but smoke still hangs in the air. I make my way into the house and burrow beneath the quilts on my bed.

Fighting sleep, I wonder what Daddy's up to, why he's not home?

"C'est Fini"

~

If only I could return to the dream, playing in Bubba's
chicken yard, me and Mabelee safe behind the green
picket fence. I'd do anything to erase last night. Did
it happen, or was it just a nightmare?

At dawn, I get a faint whiff of smoke.

And Daddy's home. In the kitchen, he looks like
he hasn't slept much, but he's reading the paper,
same as any Sunday morning. Mama seems jitterier.
When Daddy pushes away from the breakfast table,
he gives strict instructions. "I want everybody to
stay home today. Do not go anywhere."

"What about church?" I say, trying to provoke
him to talking—where did he go last night?—but he
only says to Mama, "Do something with her." Even
Mama the Methodist doesn't seem concerned about
missing church.

I try to call Mim-Mim. Busy. Duane. Busy. Finally,
Miss Blue delivers news up Kingdom Hill. "The
phones are busy this morning, won't get through till
things settle down." So the phone lines are scorched.
"What's going on?" I ask innocently, and Miss Blue
says, her corduroy old face calm as if she believes it,
"Nigs got carried away last night and burned down

their fancy school. Not surprised, are you, Silvy? The kind of thing they do best."

That old hoonch! I'm so mad, I'm quivering. She knows what really happened, and she knows I'm not surprised. Or does she?

Monday's *New Era* has a short article tucked before the classifieds. "Local Fugitives" the article is headed, and then it begins with Brother Posey asking for an investigation into the unfortunate occurrence at their school. The mayor answers, politely it says, nothing can be done since the "incident" was caused by members of Brother Posey's own congregation! Then there's mention of Mabelee and Alpha, missing, and a long description of Jefferson, saying he's an outside activist who's been known to cause trouble. No mention of the school's burning at all.

Missing?! Cause trouble?

All week, I hear what people think. Duane says it's a crying shame. His daddy told him the Negro school is a complete loss, ashes. James says he's not surprised, anything can happen here. And Mim-Mim has strict instructions: "Don't talk about it."

So, we start not talking about it, a lot.

Our big topic becomes what everyone will wear to Tinky's wedding. Turns out, those are wasted discussions.

The *New Era* informs us the wedding is off. "L'amour, C'est Fini" screams the headline in two-inch type. For a spread like that, you'd have expected a victory at the Alamo. Seems Mr. Travis Terrell Putnam flat out changed his mind. Not too diplomatically either, I hear.

Count on one thing, Miz Stookes got what she wanted—a social event to remember. Got her comedownance too. By the time Tinky's shoulda-been wedding day rolls around, most everybody acts as if everything's normal.

Spring's budding out, and there's still no school in the Bottom. And not only here. The radio says Negro schools and churches are mysteriously catching fire around the South.

I can't hold it any longer, and I question Daddy. "I know you went out that night, Daddy. The phone woke me and I saw you leave towards town. You go to the Bottom?"

"How many times do I have to tell you to stay out of this, Sis?" He holds out his hand, as if to stop me.

"Well, you got involved. Did you go with the mob and burn them out? Torch what they'd worked so hard for?"

"Is that what you think, Silvy?"

"You call 'em 'nigs' sometimes, and you said they shouldn't come over to Whitetown at night, said Jefferson was a troublemaker. Probably Alpha too."

"Whitetown?" Daddy says weakly. "Now you're talking like them. Think about yourself for a minute, Sis. You want your little friend for a playmate with no more thought than wanting a goat or a horse. What about her life? You invite Mabelee up for manners lessons to learn how *we* do? If you're honest with yourself, you may be just one step ahead of the ones carrying torches."

Daddy's words shock me, but I think about Mabelee wanting to be a cheerleader. Something as simple as a football field with real bleachers. Did I help her? Or Mabelee offering to work for me, just so she'd have good books, a real school. I wasn't even keen on helping her get out of town. She had to beg. Beg. Some friend. I remember her as a little kid sitting on the curb when I marched inside the post office for mail. I didn't think anything of it, and she never complained. Mabelee eating in the kitchen, nodding sweetly and saying "Thankee." Mabelee drinking from the spigot behind Keasler's.

It's like before and after eyeglasses. You think everything's okay, and then you see it's not. "That hurts, Daddy," I say.

"Damn right," he agrees. "Meanness always hurts."

I laughed about Lost South. I thought Alpha was lazy, that the coloreds didn't plan much. Mabelee and Jefferson and Alpha were not like me. They had guts.

"Oh, Daddy." My trickle of doubt turns everything murky. "But the night the school burned and Mabelee was here . . ."

"Mabelee? Mabelee?" he asks, repeating her name. "What was she doing over here that night?"

"She was scared and she was running. She came for help. My help."

"And?" Daddy says, his pistol eyes cocked, leaning so close I can see the whiskers coming out of his pores. "I'm sure you minded what I said and stayed out of it."

We eye each other. How can I love someone who did what I know is wrong? "Would you think hard of me, Daddy, if I told you I helped them?"

"*Them?*" Daddy says. "My daughter wouldn't do that, would she?"

The warning in his voice startles me. "Your daughter did," I admit, almost choking on the words, but knowing too I am finally speaking up. I can't go back now.

Daddy covers his eyes. "Why in God's name, Silvy? I've told you and told you, getting involved is dangerous. You could've been hurt or killed. Violence can turn on you, like that." He snaps his fingers. "Will you ever understand I'm trying to keep you safe?"

Daddy's shoulders sag, and his eyes dim. "Leave me alone, Sis. I've had about as much as I can stand. How did things get so out of hand?"

If Daddy saw Jefferson in town that night, he'd chase him, no matter who he was with. Any white man in this town would. But Daddy doesn't mention seeing him.

So maybe Mabelee and Jefferson and Alpha got away, made it out west.

Maybe . . .

"We Smile, But . . ."

Even Mim-Mim the Snoop can't find out much. She says the Negro kids are making do with Sunday school rooms for classrooms, hymnals for books. That's about all we hear. We don't find out what's going on over there.

Over here, we are afraid. Our old lives scare us. We step back a little when we talk to people we've always known—I shied away from Tub once, just a teense, but he noticed and said, "Oooh, Miss Silvy." We've begun locking our doors.

In the woods, I spy on Old Man Fulton checking his traps. I'm filled with hatred, he's so disgusting. From behind a tree, I watch him lick his finger and test the wind. Then, as he hunkers along, I wonder if he's mean 'cause he's so darn ignorant. Unkempt and pitiful, he's not like the big shot nightstalker with a torch.

Also, I see Uncle J. D. at church, family dinners, and Keasler's. With downturned mouth, he glares, his usual self, presiding over our lives. I keep my distance, same as always, and I don't even know if he was there.

Some places, white schools are closing rather than

let Negroes attend. White citizens' councils are forming—discussing, deciding—even though the Court unanimously told everyone what to do. On our school board, Daddy reassures people, saying the state will get things sorted out. He misses some board meetings 'cause he's traveling to get more Gulf stations built.

I step up practicing the piano. Forget school problems. Think sharps and flats. Miss Maggie's spring recital is coming up, right along with the tulips. I'm going to play a sappy piece called "You'll Never Walk Alone," while Larry will be playing from Mozart's *The Marriage of Figaro.*

The recital is always held at Miss Maggie's house. A black plaster servant, grinning enormously, offers a welcoming hand just outside her front door.

Mim-Mim and I stand behind Miss Maggie's velvet hallway curtain, watching the audience file into the front room. This is the first recital Bubba's attended, and she looks apprehensive. Still, she and Mama sit center front, first row. The guests are nodding pleasantly to each other when the door opens and Allie Rae slips in! Her hair's in a French twist, and she's wearing dangling earrings like her mama's. She slinks into a chair by the door.

"I can't be-*lieve* it," Mim-Mim gasps.

"I called her last night," I confess. "She said she never misses high-society events."

"She never misses anything," Mim-Mim admits.

The recital begins when Miss Maggie walks up front, heels clicking like a tap dancer's. Her hair's piled on her head, and she's wearing a crinkly dress that shows her deep-as-a-gorge cleavage. (When she sings "Texas, Our Texas," those boobies take on a life of their own.) She stands in a pool of light and taps a polished fingernail on the piano top. "Well, hello," she drawls, "we're delighted you're here. With great but humble pride, our young people present this program, 'Memories of Yesterday, Today, and Tomorrow,' for your delectable pleasure."

"Humble pride?" whispers Mim-Mim. "Doesn't make an ounce of sense."

"Hush. It's starting."

Miss Maggie announces, "We'll begin our afternoon's entertainment with Master James Van Tummel's rendition of 'The Song of the Volga Boatmen.'" Barely five years old, little J. V. T. walks out. He begins. And balks. And begins again. By now, everyone's straining with the boatmen to get that skiff through the water. J. V. T. sniffles softly and slides off the stool.

I know just how he feels, and my piece isn't up for a while.

A few more students, representing memories of yesterday, parade out: Miz Herman's neighbor, Louise; Miz Ellason's niece, Raye-Baby; and Jackson Fulton, who, true to Fulton style, forgets his number halfway through. He shrugs but doesn't seem to mind. Bubba says all those Fultons are born tired and raised lazy. Some people nod off. Allie Rae yawns loudly.

Mama and Bubba look so proud when Larry comes to the piano. He transfixes the audience with Mozart, and the women rise in unison, clapping, at his finish. Larry ducks behind the curtain. Miss Maggie says, "That was just precious, Larry. Thank you, oh, thank you. Now, our next number will be brought to us by Miss Minerva Goodwin, who has worked long and hard on her presentation. Minerva."

"That's Mim-Mim, hyphenated," Mim-Mim mutters through clenched teeth. "My number comes from the memories of today, al-tho-ugh, it's hard for me to understand how a memory can be a memory if it's still today."

Miss Maggie rushes to stand beside the piano bench. She looks hard at Mim-Mim, who's seated herself and straightened her new pearl collar. "What Minerva means is that . . . ." Miss Maggie stalls; perhaps "memories of tomorrow" has just dawned on her. "What Minerva really means is that she has practiced so-oooo hard on this piece, I am certain it will become a beautiful memory of today." She pauses. "Minerva, dear, whenever you're ready."

Mim-Mim shakes her head, and her hair fans nicely down her back. She poises her hands above the keyboard like Liberace. "Well," she yells, "a one, a two, a three to go, Mama, and that's aw right. . . ." She pounds out Elvis's song and makes that piano rock.

Mama actually jumps in her seat. Then she smiles. When she looks at Bubba, her smile vanishes instantly.

Mim-Mim's "That's All Right, Mama" sounds as though her life depends on it. She stomps her feet on the floor. A porcelain dish, two cupped hands fringed with lace, bounces on the piano.

Miss Maggie looks at the notes in her palm, checking, and then at the piano in disbelief. Soon, the whole room moves with one rolling motion. Feet tap, heads bob, fingers click. Mim-Mim crouches, bent at half-mast, playing. She wiggles and she sings; she yips for accent.

Leafie peeks through the kitchen door. She watches the performance, beating the rhythm on the doorjamb. "You tell 'em, girl, lay your burden down."

Miss Maggie frowns at Leafie and motions her head toward the kitchen. Leafie ignores her, tapping her foot.

When Mim-Mim finishes playing, the room settles down, and she lowers her head the way you do if you don't want to laugh in church. Mim-Mim probably feels that performance will get her started toward stardom. It gets her noticed all right.

The afternoon has turned the color of old newspaper. Not a sound comes from the room. Then somebody murmurs, "Looks like that girl made a evolutionary U-turn somewheres," and Allie Rae adds loud enough for all to hear, "Yeah. Wadn't it great?"

Like a windup toy, Miss Maggie walks over and switches on the light.

Mim-Mim stands, holds out her skirt, and dips into a curtsy she learned at the School of Manners. She bats her eyelids and smiles at Allie Rae.

Eyes narrowing, Miss Maggie winces and says, as if dismissing a gnat, "That will do nicely, Minerva."

"You're welcome, I'm sure." When Mim-Mim passes me, Allie Rae on her heels, she says, "Meet us out back when it's over." She slams the door, but not as hard as she could.

"Well, I'll swan," Miss Maggie says, "working with young people these days is *such* a challenge. They're changing so fast." Her voice goes up jauntily, and she nods at me. "I think we'll move along to your sweet piece."

At the piano, I arrange my skirt, hands shaking. The keys swim before my eyes. I know my piece backward and forward but cannot remember how it begins. I look at Mama who mouths, "Be sweet."

I can't remember a single note, but still, be sweet!

"Dum de dum, dum de dum, dum de dum, dum, dum." Miss Maggie begins humming my tune, her talc-y bosom rising. She says my piece will end on an inspirational note and give everyone courage— for tomorrow, I suppose.

Right here in front of me, Mama and Bubba look like they could use an inspirational note. "I need to announce a slight change in the program," I hear myself say as I rise from the piano bench.

Miss Maggie grabs her heart; she clasps her hands on her ample chest. Astonishment seems to be her main emotion. She looks nothing like an etiquette teacher.

"'We Wear the Mask,'" I begin, "by Paul Laurence Dunbar. A Negro poet." I'm not even sure where the words come from; I'd read the poem so often, remembering Mabelee, they are just there.

> We wear the mask that grins and lies,
> It hides our cheeks and shades our eyes,—
> This debt we pay to human guile;
> With torn and bleeding hearts we smile,
> And mouth with myriad subtleties.

Miss Maggie raises her eyeballs; her lips move. Mama and Bubba are about a stanza away from a breakdown.

> Why should the world be over-wise,
> In counting all our tears and sighs?
> Nay, let them only see us, while
> We wear the mask.

I pause, the words haunting me. Then, I charge ahead.

> We smile, but, O great Christ, our cries
> To thee from tortured souls arise.
> We sing, but oh the clay is vile

Beneath our feet, and long the mile;
But let the world dream otherwise,
We wear the mask!

I use my arms for emphasis, and at one point,
fold my hands in prayer. By the poem's end, 'most
everyone looks angry. Mama and Bubba share startled expressions. From the back of the room comes,
"I can't believe this. Not from our Silvy."

"What's all that mean?" asks Miz Herman.

Bubba clears her throat. "It's poetry. Nigra poetry."

"Sounds like nig talk to me," puts in Miz Fulton,
and Mama answers her sweetly, "Try literary talk."

Miss Maggie fingers her necklace. "I'd like to
compliment you on a memorable presentation," she
says with slight hesitation. "And, uh, thank you for
coming."

I take that as a dismissal and scoot out back
to find Mim-Mim and Allie Rae. They're sitting on
Miss Maggie's new bomb shelter, the "in" thing
for 1955. Mim-Mim has applied white lipstick and
makeup. If it rains, she'll smear.

"How'd it go?" she asks, her head beating out
some distant rhythm.

"I messed up," I groan. "Completely forgot my
piece, so I substituted a poem." I don't say who wrote
it; they'll hear soon enough.

"You did not!" Mim-Mim says, grinning.

"Hey, Silvy. You?" Allie Rae says, "Oh, ho!" Was
she glad I forgot or happy I surprised everyone?

"At least I did *some*thing, Allie Rae, maybe a decent poem recital."

"Did she say anything about me after I left?" Mim-Mim asks, sullenly.

"Only something about young people being *such* a challenge these days. Changing so fast. I think she meant, um, hormones."

"Well, she should know with *those* dinners," Allie Rae whoops, putting her fists under her blouse and making huge boobies.

That cracks us all up. Allie Rae is back!

"I needed to break away," says Mim-Mim. "You know, the real me."

"Was that the real you back there?" I ask.

"Oh, I hope so. I get so tired of just going along."

Just going along. "What made you do it?"

"I really think it was the Minerva thing, over and over. I *had* to do it."

"Don't worry about it. Lots of people change their tunes," says Allie Rae, "and it's not like it's Hollywood. Though I'd say, Mim-Mim, you'll do pretty good out there in Tinseltown."

Relief washes over Mim-Mim's face. "Yeah?"

"Yeah," I agree. People change their tunes. But when someone changes *anything,* it changes everything. Like Daddy says, changing times can make people dangerous.

Just look at our town.

"The Hindquarters of Bad Luck"

I'm invisible in my own town. In Spring Park, the
McAdams sisters are sitting on their bench. I wave
and call, "Mornin' Miss Clara, Miss Hattie," but
they keep sitting, oh so quiet.

Same thing on Main Street, nobody speaks. The
post office comes to a complete stop when I go in.
Everyone stares at me. Finally the postmaster asks,
"Any books coming in today, Silvy, poetry books?"
His snide tone chills me.

"No sir," I say as polite as I can muster, and scram.

Outside, catching my breath, I hear "You'll Never
Walk Alone," the recital piece I should've played,
starting in my head. "When you walk through
a storm, hold your head up high." And that's what
I decide to do.

Allie Rae thinks what I did at Miss Maggie's is
the funniest thing she ever heard. "That ol' heifer'll
need a mask her ownself before showing her face on
Main Street anytime soon," she says. On the way to
the football field, she jumps and does a split in the
air. "Gimme a D!" she screams. "Gimme a U! Gimme
an N! Gimme a D-U-N-B-A-R!!! *Goooooooooo*, Silvy!!"
She's cracking up me and Mim-Mim.

There's good news at home too. Daddy tells Mama he's got gas stations scheduled to open, and he can't be worrying about piano recitals gone wrong. He thinks I've had enough of Miss Maggie's! Mama agrees and says I'd better get to know Emily Dickinson quick and stick with her.

A week later, I leave school a little late. A blustery, cutting wind warns that it's almost storm season in Tornado Alley. Bubba's car is parked in our side yard. Funny she didn't stop by school and carry me home.

Inside, everyone is sitting around the dining room. Whoa, I think, the whole family gathered like a wake. "Sorry I'm a little late."

"We waited," Mama says. "Your daddy has something to tell us all."

Uh-oh, my daddy. They're in it together. I get a terrible feeling then. Daddy scans the room, his eyes not lighting till he gets to Bubba. "I'm sorry," he begins, so softly I have to strain to hear. "We've hit the hindquarters of bad luck. My new stations aren't going to open. At least, not with me as consignee." He looks exhausted. "Remember Mr. Jacobs, from Houston?"

Wind rattles the windowpanes.

I remember Mr. Jacobs all right, the big shot who prayed in public. "Wasn't he the one who said what a good job you were doing?" I ask. "How they couldn't get along without you?"

"One and the same," Daddy says, rubbing his

hand down his cheek. "Right when the stations are finished, Mr. Jacobs ups and changes tunes." Daddy slams his hand on the chair arm. "Now Jacobs says, 'No damn consignee in some flea-bitten town is going to make more money than me.'" Daddy stands, pointing his finger at his chest. "*I'm* the damn consignee, and Jacobs is a man without principles."

Bubba flinches, probably more from "damn" than the news.

"That's not fair!" I cry. "You earned that money, or will earn it when the new stations open."

"Nobody ever said life is fair, Sis. The bottom line," Daddy sighs, "is that Jacobs is taking our stations and putting them under the consignee in Gilmer. Upshur County. Lock, stock, and barrel. And that fella hasn't done a thing to deserve it. Not a blasted thing."

I'm so mad I could spit.

"It'll still be a good-enough job, won't it?" Larry mumbles, inventorying the room for a nod. "Without the new stations?" Sara jams her fingers in her ears.

Like weeds, Daddy's silver hair has overgrown the black. "Good enough for some maybe, but not for me, son. That brings us to this talk, here. Your mama thinks we could do better elsewhere. Good schools, the works. I think she might have a point. California would be a fresh start."

Bubba pushes herself up from the table with her knuckles. "I knew it," she mutters. "California! What you'd expect."

"Mother, please, this is hard enough as it is, but I don't want my kids to grow up in the middle of cultural *and* economic meanness," Mama says softly. "It'll be new lessons in a new place."

"I'm sorry," Daddy says when Bubba lurches away. "You know I wouldn't hurt you for the world."

Mama nods.

"You've both got a strange way of showing it," Bubba rasps, heading out into the wind.

I swallow hard, watching our family unravel.

Bubba looked so hurt. What will she do without us? Nobody else will ride around with her on Sunday afternoons the way she drives. "You can't make me move," I announce. "This is where I belong, where my people are, either put under or walking around."

Mama's response is quick. "We're your people and we're going to California." Her voice is barbed-wire sharp.

"It's not fair, Mama. I'll never ever have friends like this again." Their faces blur before me like pictures in the yearbook: Allie Rae, Mim-Mim, Duane, and James. Mabelee's picture isn't there. I have to face it. She's gone.

"I'm doing good in school too. And I can even play a sharp or flat sometimes on that stupid piano. Best of all, I've got a good chance of making cheerleader. It's plain not fair."

Mama pulls me to her and pushes my hair out of my eyes. Her voice softens. "Why do you always go kicking and screaming when anything's new? You might like California, honey. Lots of beaches, an ocean, mountains. I read in the *Dallas Morning News* that Mr. Walt Disney is building a new entertainment park out there called Disneyland. It's unlike anything you can imagine."

"Mama, it can't be half as good as the State Fair," I say. "Nothing is."

Mama shakes her head. "Don't be so provincial. The world does not revolve around Texas."

For me it does. "Well, I'm not going I tell you."

"We Need to Pony Up"

The wind whooshes 'round Kingdom Hill at first light. It seeps through the walls and causes my wallpaper to breathe in and out. My stomach flip-flops remembering yesterday's news. California! I'd never fit in out there.

An article has miraculously appeared overnight on my nightstand. It's about Mr. Walt Disney and his big amusement-park plans. He's spending millions. Paper says it's grander than anything anywheres. Fantasyland, Tomorrowland, Frontierland, Adventureland. And guess what? They'll even have Main Street! Bet Mr. Disney would be surprised to know we've had all that for years in Hughes Springs.

At the breakfast table, Mama and Daddy have gone into overdrive, planning. Mama has stacks of lists much like Brother Posey's, only hers are what we'll give away, what we'll pack. A chilly thought hits me. Mabelee didn't get to take a thing. When Mama and Daddy see me, they put on the brakes.

"Then you're serious? You're leaving every-*thing,* every*body* I love?" I shout. "Californians eat funny food, talk fast. We'd be running around with Yankees."

"Watch it, Silvy," Daddy warns. "I mean it this time."

"This is what we have to do," Mama says, putting her papers in order, moving on. "Next week your daddy is leaving for Los Angeles to look for work. Lots of opportunities there. When he finds something, we'll join him. And Silvy, being the oldest, I expect you to set an example."

"For an example, you can count me O-U-T out!"

"Listen Sis," Daddy says, "don't break your mama's heart. We're in this together, as a family. Got that?"

"My family lives in Texas. And I'm 101 percent Texan." I put my head on the kitchen table and cry so hard I sound like Mama. She rubs my shoulders. "It'll be okay, honey."

"It would be so hard, Mama."

"I know that, Silvy, I know. Why don't you call Allie Rae and Mim-Mim and talk to them? Maybe they'll make you feel better." Mama doesn't have a clue. I need to talk to them all right, but not to tell what she thinks.

We plan to meet at Spring Park. Leaving home, I start memorizing Kingdom Hill—oak tree, blackberry brambles, magnolia tree, red dirt. I'll be somewheres in Texas, that's certain, but not on Kingdom Hill. Before I've gotten past Miss Blue's, purple and chartreuse clouds churn overhead. This is part of our Adventureland: one minute it's pretty, the next we're blowing away.

Allie Rae and Mim-Mim are sitting in the spring-house watching the sky. "This better be good, Silvy," Allie Rae says. "That storm could be serious."

My heart takes a dive toward San Antonio. I've got to tell them my family's moving. I start with Daddy's losing his job. "Do you think my poem recital could've caused it?" I ask. Much the way Jefferson's new school infuriated people, I think.

"Don't be silly," Allie Rae says. "Lots of people lose jobs, and they don't know a line of poetry. It just happens. He'll find something else."

"Here's the awful part. They're planning to move to Los Angeles."

"Awful?" Mim-Mim says, her eyes popping like a tadpole's. "*You're* going to Hollywood?"

"Not me. Them. I'm staying here. Maybe run away. I'll get a tent and camp on Trammel's Trace. Y'all can sneak me food and stuff."

"Girl, you two kinds of crazy?" Allie Rae asks, rolling her eyes. "Ugh—wolves, snakes, bugs. How long you think you'd last out there? Get serious. Moving's not so bad. I've done it loads. It'll be like turning your underpants."

Mim-Mim slaps her forehead. "Say what?"

No matter where Allie Rae goes, she's never far from undies. Putting 'em under, putting 'em on.

"'Member the time we went to the MYF sleepover in Gladewater," Allie Rae continues, "and we got so excited we left our overnight bags in Fellowship

Hall? Next morning, that snooty hostess over there says, 'All you young ladies brushed your teeth, changed your undies?' And Silvy looked that ol' priss eyeball-to-eyeball and says, ever so sweetly, 'Yessum, we changed 'em good.'" Allie Rae stomps her foot and brays.

Sure as one star's on our Texas flag, that'd be what Allie Rae would remember. Fifty years down the road my name will come up, and she'll say, "Oh yeah, Silvy Lane, Most Likely to Turn Her Underpants."

"Exactly what's turning undies got to do with California?" I ask weakly.

"You'd make do," Allie Rae says. "Turn those drawers and keep on going."

I feel the sobs starting again. "This isn't funny. I won't get to make cheerleader with y'all next year. We worked so hard."

Allie Rae taps my shoulder. "In case you haven't noticed, you're a little different, Silvy. You'd fit in okay out there. Lotta poetry readers and singers. Some sound colored too, like Elv—"

Mim-Mim shoots her a look. "Silvy'd be fine in California with the movie stars."

"Easy for you to say." I brush tears off my cheeks. "I'd be running my freckled self around in a bathing suit. You'd get to grow up here."

Allie Rae huffs, "No one *ever* grows up in Texas!"

"Horsefeathers," Mim-Mim says, winking at me. "You'd be okay, Silvy. I feel it in my bones. It's us who'd be bogged down in corny dogs and spring recitals." She lifts her face just like in the movies. "I, for one, would really, truly miss you."

Allie Rae handles mushiness about as well as Lester Fulton handles worms. "Girls, we need to pony up. And we better get outta here. That wind sounds like a death rattle."

As quick as it started, the storm zooms north. "Bet this is the only state in the whole forty-eight where you can actually watch the weather change," Allie Rae says. "Here it comes, there it goes. Gotta go myself, help Carlton print funeral notices."

"See you," Mim-Mim says, and when Allie Rae leaves, she turns to me. "You didn't mean that silly stuff about running off, did you? Think about it. Out on the trace you could pick daffodils all day and dodge Old Man Fulton and his hunting dogs all night. What a life."

I know I've got to figure out my Tomorrowland. "My plans are iffy as the weather, Mim-Mim."

Remember Me Kindly

Mim-Mim's right. I couldn't live on the trace. Still I begin hiking there to get flowers for Bubba. I stomp along and imagine I'm walking in the pirate Trammel's footsteps. He once buried treasure here. It is so beautiful today. Daffodils bob everywhere. Solid gold splashes over hills and into gullies. Some people think the yellow flowers are Trammel's treasure. Every spring we help Bubba pick them for Bom's urns. Since she's my best bet to stay in Texas, I pick like I have a quota.

Heading to Bubba's, I meet Goldie. Her face brightens. "Silvy! Guess what? Got me a letter from Mabelee. My girl's okay, doing right fine she says. Alpha too."

My insides shift, a little like the sidewalk when I got new glasses. "That is SO great, Goldie. Where is she?" Let it be California! If I ever visit there, maybe I'll get another chance to be a better friend. Nobody'd notice our color where everyone's tanned as Cochise.

"Couldn't rightly make it out. Wish I could write her how we're rebuilding our school. Painting a new sign. Ever'thing. But one thing sure, I'll never forget how you helped Mabelee. Never, ever. You and your daddy both."

"Daddy?!"

"Oh, yes, Silvy. Mr. Jack, he saw Mabelee, Alpha, and Jefferson trying to break in the calaboose, for some funny reason. He took 'em into Keasler's, and him and Mr. Hank hid 'em. Like you said, they left on the night train. I wouldn't of minded if Mr. Jack let 'em catch Jefferson, but he helped him out too."

So Mabelee hadn't spent time in the calaboose after all. And that phone call must've been from Uncle Hank. His apartment would have a good view of the mob forming on Main Street. He and Daddy kept Mabelee safe.

"Thank you, Goldie, for letting me know."

Maybe Mabelee'll be happier starting someplace new. I only hope she'll remember me kindly.

At Bubba's, I go 'round back to the rose garden. Bubba is unwrapping her Peace rose, removing the oak-leaves mulch from its newspaper collar.

She never looks up. I may as well have stayed on the trace, the way she concentrates on that rose. "Oak leaves don't deteriorate, they last the winter," she advises herself.

"Hey, Bubba, I brought you something."

She keeps removing the mulch, mumbling. Is she talking flower talk to her garden? Certainly not speaking to me.

I raise my voice, "I *hope* you'll *like* what I got you."

She turns slowly in my direction. Her eyes are fierce, the blue veins visible in her temples. "Look who's here," she says, the welcome in the idea, but certainly not in fact. "It's good to see one of my people walking toward me for a change. Seems like I always see them leaving, for California." She bends back over that rose with a vengeance. A flower named Peace never had it tougher.

I feel light-headed as a lifetime puzzle is verified. So the Missing Man did go to California? "What happened to my grandfather, Bubba?" She keeps jerking the rose's collar, loosening it, but Peace is fighting the good fight. "He's my people too, you know."

She says, enunciating slowly, "Sister, if he was still around, you'd be dancing your legs off in Spring Park. The 'Two Step,' 'Cotton-eyed Joe,' your dance card plumb full. You're like him in some ways."

A fun, dancing grandfather? "Tell me, please. Was he handsome? Tall? Did he have stories to tell?"

"Slow down, Silvy, you make me dizzy. To answer, he was tall and dark as a movie star, a bit of an actor, a bit of a gaming man. He was a little like your daddy. Only in his case, he was an oil rigger. Couldn't stay put. He went out west, always chancing the next oil strike."

I can't stand the thought of my grandfather, someone like me, leaving Bubba to go west. No wonder she thinks Papa hung the moon; he's the only man she trusts.

"Why didn't you go with him?"

She looks startled. "He asked me to, but *leave* Hughes Springs? I could never leave my people."

What about me leaving? I'm her people too. "Bubba, can I stay here with you?"

She looks like she might faint. She sits flat on the ground and puts her head between her knees. When she recovers, she answers thoughtfully, "No, Silvan, you belong with your mama and daddy. And you're tougher than me. Your mama too." She pauses. "I know she's trying to do what's right. She's also scared 'cause she doesn't want her kids trapped here."

I look at Bubba. Suddenly, I see how much my people make me, me. And they're mostly good people. They really are. But something got messed up a long time ago that can get us on the wrong side of right sometimes. That's all I can figure. Why does it take a school burning before I can see?

As much as I want to stay in Texas, California *might* be interesting, even adventurous. I'd get to start over, like Mabelee. Perhaps someone out west in turned underpants is sniffing around, sharing my love of horse sweat. It's not like I have to go there and like it. Or be sweet.

Bubba removes her gardening gloves, stuffs them in her pockets. "Bless your heart. These daffodils will look so pretty in Mama's old urns. I'm much obliged. Say now, Silvan," she says, all inspired, "your grandfather gave me a few good gifts before he left."

"As good as the daffodils?"

She laughs. "Better. Gifts like you and your mama, Larry and Sara—best gifts a gal could get."

Well, is this peculiar, or what? Mama's right. Life gets you back when you're not looking. Here I sit on a fine spring day discussing doing *it* with my grandmother!

"How about you and me having ourselves a treat? Co-Colas and Hershey bars keep you tough," she says, the old hospitality back in her voice.

"That sounds great," I say, thinking, who knows— maybe horses *can* go to parties in California?

L. KING PÉREZ remains 101 percent Texan, although she lives on a wooded hill in her beloved adopted Ohio with her husband, Jess. Her passions are grandparenting, working for the environment, and introducing young people to the power of words; her hobbies include gardening, cooking, and reading. Ms. Pérez enjoys hosting dinner parties, trying new recipes and wines, driving vintage cars, walking Jack Russell terriers with attitude, placing feral cats (Spot, you go, girl), and planting wildflowers and trees. *Remember As You Pass Me By* is a historical novel based partly on personal experiences. She serves as president of the Dunbareans at the Paul Laurence Dunbar State Memorial in Dayton, Ohio, and she and her husband divide their time between Ohio and San Miguel de Allende, Mexico, an artists' colony conducive to writing.

Acknowledgments

Special thanks to my husband Jess, with whom I've shared the rallying cry "Remember the Alamo!" for over forty years, and our children, John and Lissa Toney Pérez, who inspire me. To my parents, N. A. King and Enid Carter King, brother Terry King and sister Jane King Mazzoni for lots of material. To Paul Laurence Dunbar, who dared to be great, for literary inspiration, and to the Dunbareans and staff at the Paul Laurence Dunbar State Memorial for guidance. To my wonderful agent Edy Selman who encourages, encourages, encourages her writers to keep the faith and to Ben Barnhart, an editor with vision who worked diligently to make this book better. And my dedicated Texan English teacher Ernestelle Berry who instilled in her students the knowledge that anything is possible, but with good grammar please. To friends who offered loving support: Mainly, Marybeth Lorbiecki!!! Annette Brazeale, Dan Bushong, Jill Buzzard, Vicki Dehnert, Morgan Mazzoni Dent, Diane Dalloway DeWall, Ann and Peter Duffield, Toni de Gerez, Lisa Evans, Chris Frapwell, Jolene Graham, Amy Grogan, Cheryl Hacker, Don Hooser, Phoebe Hunt, the late Dr. M. T. "Pepper" Jenkins, Henry King, Ruth Knight, Judy Kocher,

Lavonne Maroney, Mary Louise McKaughan, Thelma
Miller, Gail Newmark, The Read 'n Feed Book Club,
Jenny Ruiz, Paula Schanilec, Leonore Sonnenschein,
Annemarie Smith, Carole Solomon, Kathy Tirschek,
and reference librarians everywhere, particularly
Jackie at Wright Memorial Library. Special kudos
to Nadja, Mirjana, and Dmitri Mataya, junior read-
ers with sharp eyes. One more time to Marybeth
Lorbiecki who saw potential from the get-go and
never let up. That girl is gentle as wildflowers,
tenacious as a snapping turtle waiting for thunder.
Thank you all. I mean it now, you hear?

HISTORICAL FICTION FOR YOUNG READERS

To order books or for more information, contact
Milkweed at (800) 520-6455
or visit our Web site (www.milkweed.org).

The $66 Summer
John Armistead

Milkweed Prize for Children's Literature
New York Public Library Best Books of the Year:
"Books for the Teen Age"

A story of interracial friendships in the segregation-
era South.

The Return of Gabriel
John Armistead

A story of Freedom Summer.

The Trouble with Jeremy Chance
George Harrar

Bank Street College Best Children's Books of the Year

Father-son conflict during the final days of World
War I.

Hard Times for Jake Smith
Aileen Kilgore Henderson

A girl searches for her family in the Depression-era
South.

MORE HISTORICAL FICTION FOR YOUNG READERS

I Am Lavina Cumming
Susan Lowell
Mountains & Plains Booksellers Association Award

This lively story culminates with the 1906 San Francisco earthquake.

The Secret of the Ruby Ring
Yvonne MacGrory

A blend of time travel and historical fiction set in 1885 Ireland.

A Bride for Anna's Papa
Isabel R. Marvin

Milkweed Prize for Children's Literature

Life on Minnesota's Iron Range in the early 1900s.

Behind the Bedroom Wall
Laura E. Williams

Milkweed Prize for Children's Literature
Jane Addams Peace Award Honor Book

Tells a story of the Holocaust through the eyes of a young girl.

CONTEMPORARY FICTION FOR YOUNG READERS

Trudy
Jessica Lee Anderson

Milkweed Prize for Children's Literature

Reveals the upheaval Alzheimer's brings to a young girl's family.

Perfect
Natasha Friend

Milkweed Prize for Children's Literature

A thirteen-year-old girl struggles with bulimia after her father dies.

No Place
Kay Haugaard

Based on a true story of Latino youth who create an inner-city park.

The Summer of the Pike
Jutta Richter

A young girl helps her friends cope with their mother's illness as they search for the elusive pike.

MILKWEED EDITIONS

Founded in 1979, Milkweed Editions is one of the largest independent, nonprofit literary publishers in the United States. Milkweed publishes with the intention of making a humane impact on society, in the belief that good writing can transform the human heart and spirit. Within this mission, Milkweed publishes in four areas: fiction, nonfiction, poetry, and children's literature for middle-grade readers.

JOIN US

Milkweed depends on the generosity of foundations and individuals like you, in addition to the sales of its books. In an increasingly consolidated and bottom-line-driven publishing world, your support allows us to select and publish books on the basis of their literary quality and the depth of their message. Please visit our Web site (www.milkweed.org) or contact us at (800) 520-6455 to learn more about our donor program.

Interior design by Wendy Holdman
Typeset in Apollo
by Stanton Publication Services
Printed on acid-free Rolland Enviro paper
by Friesens Corporation (100% postconsumer waste)